UNINVITED GUEST

Trouble struck the schooner Griselda at 9:40 on an April evening. It was not the fault of the weather or the sea or the soundness of her hull. The trouble was human. A woman. Her name was Julia Parks, though in the beginning she insisted it was Lambert.

It was hard to blame Howard Crane for bringing her aboard, because Julia always got what she wanted. What she wanted in this case was money. Keith Lambert's— her ex-husband's—money. That there were others too who wanted it was one of the first things that came to the minds of the Barbados police the next morning when Julia was found suffocated in her cabin. But the only trail they had to follow was one of tangled lives and tangled motives that led to jealousy, blackmail, native secrecy, and sudden death—all against the peaceful tropical background of picturesque Barbados.

Here is another of the highly polished, tightly knit, and suspenseful mysteries that have made George Harmon Coxe for almost twenty years one of the deans of mystery writers.

GEORGE HARMON COXE

Uninvited Guest

WILDSIDE PRESS

UNINVITED GUEST

1

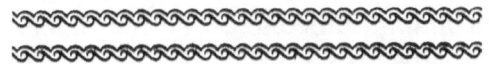

TROUBLE struck the schooner *Griselda* at 9:40 on an April evening. It was not the fault of the weather or the sea or the soundness of her hull; for the sea was flat, the weather calm, and the *Griselda* was moored a hundred-odd yards off the Royal Barbados Yacht Club and about an equal distance diagonally from the Aquatic Club pier.

The trouble was human. A woman. Her name was Julia Parks, though in the beginning she insisted it was Lambert.

The British West Indies Airways plane which brought her from San Juan touched down at Seawell Airport at 6:20, and she remained in her seat until her fellow passengers had cleared the aisle. Then she stood up on the sloping floor, tucking her yellow-blond hair under her close-fitting hat and pulling her suit skirt round on her hips until it hung straight. She buttoned her jacket, tugged it down, picked up her vanity case and took a last look at the rack overhead. At the door the hostess handed over her coat and then she was going down the steps and feeling again the soft warm breeze that swept in so constantly from the sea.

She stood a moment on the concrete ramp, breathing deeply and letting the breeze cool her hot moist face. Down the coast at South Point the lighthouse winked at her in the gathering dusk, and as she walked towards the coral-stone terminal building she could see the parked cars and hear the welcoming shouts directed at others who had preceded her. Approaching the door marked *Incoming*, someone called her name. When she glanced up Howard Crane waved to her from the embankment beyond the wire enclosure.

The interior of the lighted building was almost bare of furniture and, at the moment, crowded. There were two or three raised desks, temporarily presided over by uniformed officials, a couple of benches, a long customs counter bisecting the room. A tall Negro sergeant, immaculate in blue-black trousers with red stripes, white jacket, white pith helmet, and polished Sam Browne belt, served as a walking information bureau to the milling passengers but Julia had been through this before and knew exactly what to do.

A line had already formed at the immigration desk and she shoved in ahead of an elderly man who was fumbling in his wallet for some identification. The uniformed official gave her a questioning look but silently accepted the identity card the airline had given her in New York, and her driver's license.

"Where will you be staying?" he asked when he had checked her name on the manifest.

"At the Carib."

"And how long do you plan to be with us?"

"Oh, probably only a few days."

"You have your reservation on a return flight?"

"A ticket, but no reservation. I'll see about it tomorrow."

"Is someone meeting you?"

The heat had begun to work on her again. She could feel the perspiration coming and the soft-voiced but persistent questioning annoyed her.

"Mr. Howard Crane," she said impatiently.

"Very good." The man returned her card and license and waved her towards the customs counter.

The bags had been trucked in from the plane and Julia quickly identified her own. She gave her name to the customs man and he found her declaration, glanced at it, asked her to sign it. When she did so he gave her another form on which she wrote down the amount of currency she was carrying.

"No English pounds?" he asked when she had estimated her cash.

"None."

He gave her the form after he had torn off a voucher at the bottom, explaining that she must turn the form in when she left the island. Then, not bothering to open her bags, he chalk-marked them, signaled to a porter, and presently she was outside in the street where a mixed crowd—white, brown, and black—waited for relatives and friends.

Howard Crane, who had been watching her progress through an open window, tipped the porter and told him where to put the bags, and now Julia gave him both her hands, coming up on tiptoe to give him a perfunctory kiss, hearing him say something about her looking fit and that he had engaged a room for her at the Carib Hotel.

She said that was fine. She said she was glad to be here and it was sweet of him to meet her. But even as she spoke her glance slid beyond him to the low frame building across the street that served as the airport bar and restaurant. At the moment she felt hot, tired, and dirty. She'd been in her clothes ever since the evening before and she wanted very much to have a bath as quickly as she could. Yet, in spite of the fact that she'd had two whisky and sodas on the flight down from the last stop in Antigua, she felt the need of another even more than she needed the bath.

For now that she was actually in Barbados the tension which had been building slowly ever since she left New York was making itself felt. She was nerved-up, jittery, and impatient, and it annoyed her that she should feel this way. She was well aware that this trip might be the biggest gamble she had ever taken, but she had assessed the odds before she started. She understood the difficulties of her scheme as well as its importance to her, and having flown all night and most of the day she was determined to carry on, secure in the knowledge that if she were successful she would have more money in her hands than she'd ever had in her life.

Crane was at once agreeable when she suggested the drink, and so they climbed the steps and found a corner table in the bare and uninviting building. The order given, she took off her hat and began to work on her hair.

"Good trip?" Crane asked.

"Horrible."

"Rough?"

"No, not that. Just leaving New York before midnight and getting into San Juan at some ungodly hour in the morning when nothing's open but the immigration and customs."

She spoke past the bobby-pin in her mouth, tucked it in place and surveyed the result in her compact mirror. She patted the shine off her cheeks and, screwing her mouth up, began to work on it with her lipstick, her words distorted as she continued.

"Check your bags and it's too early to shop and there's no place to go for breakfast but the Hilton, and then sit around dying on the vine until it's two o'clock and you can get the plane out."

Crane grinned. He said there was a nice bar in the San Juan airport.

"Once it finally opens, yes."

Julia put her make-up things away and snapped her bag shut. When the drinks came and she'd had a large swallow she gave Crane her attention.

"Your wife away again?"

"Jamaica."

"For long?"

"Another fortnight."

"Having fun?"

Crane tipped one hand. "I always have fun."

Julia pushed a stray wisp of blond hair back from her forehead and watched him with heavy-lidded eyes, speculating, knowing that what Crane said was true. Seeing again his tanned, blunt-jawed face with its gray eyes and thinning gray-brown hair, the deep wrinkles that creased his forehead laterally and came from scowling against the sun, she knew that he had made something of a career of fun for quite some years. As her mind went on she remembered other things as well.

The Crane family had been on the island for generations, first as planters and later, when hard times took most of their property, as proprietors of a small grocery store on Roebuck Street. Howard, now in his early forties, still had an inactive interest in the store but mostly he attended to a variety of small enterprises, the principal one being a modern and rather exclusive residential club on the leeward coast. He kept a few horses and raced them at the tri-yearly meets. He had a small sloop which he sailed occasionally, and he was one of the best tennis players on the island. But the important thing, Julia knew, was that all this was possible because of Crane's wife, an English girl ten years his junior, who happened to be not only attractive, but wealthy.

Julia understood that when Mrs. Crane was in town Howard paid attention. When she was away it was different. Last summer for instance, when Mrs. Crane had been in England and Julia's own marriage had foundered. Howard had been fun then. He liked a good time, was attractive to women and was always ready to go to a party or give one. There was, she remembered, a word for people like Howard. She thought it was gregarious. But this time it would be different. Such things as parties could wait. This trip was strictly business and again she gave the matter her attention.

"And what's my husband doing with his new inheritance?"

"You mean your ex-husband, don't you?" Crane hesitated and Julia did not correct him. "Spending it," he said, and chuckled, though his eyes were no longer at ease.

"On what?"

"Various things."

"I was afraid of that."

"As a matter of fact, if you'd come a day later you would have missed him."

"Missed him?" Julia frowned. "How?"

"You remember the Farrows?"

"I remember *her*. Vivian. A tall, black-haired number. Married to some Englishman, isn't she?" She paused while an undertone of scorn grew in her voice. "The ex-show girl pretending she's a lady. Sure I remember. What about them?"

"They've chartered a schooner. They're off on a ten-day cruise in the morning. Keith is going along."

Julia reached for her glass and found it empty. Wanting another drink but not wanting to show it, she pushed it aside and gathered her things, a little panicky in spite of herself as the thought of failure struck at her and she considered the penalty of any such miscalculation. Suppose Keith *had* gone. Suppose— She dismissed the thought angrily, her painted mouth a tight unpleasant line. She shook her head and concentrated on her smile.

Keith was still here and that was what mattered. There was money to be had here and there in Barbados and she was going to get some of it, one way or another. If she had to resort to threats and be generally obnoxious in the process she was prepared to act accordingly. If other means were necessary she would make them up as she went along.

"A cruise?" she said. "That's interesting."

She paused again, thinking, aware that he was watching her. When she looked at him he seemed to be relaxed and at ease, all except the gray eyes. The half smile on his mouth did not seem to touch his gaze and deep down there was a certain nervousness and uncertainty, as though he was not entirely happy in her company. Or was the impression only a product of her imagination? She shrugged the thought aside by telling herself she did not particularly care whether he was happy or not. Howard Crane had a place in her plans and there were many things he could tell her. For the moment, however, all that could wait.

"Have you any plans?"

"Plans?"

"I mean now," she said. "Or for this evening?"

"No."

"Then I'll tell you what we might do. When I get straightened out at the Carib we could have a couple of drinks, and dinner, and"—she touched his hand —"maybe a brandy. Then I'd like to take a look at this schooner."

2

ABOARD the *Griselda,* Alan Scott busied himself in the main cabin, making sure there was plenty of liquid refreshment on the sideboard when the party who had chartered the schooner came back from dinner at the Club Morgan for a nightcap. A lanky, easy-moving man in his late twenties, he had a longish, angular face, wide in the mouth but with a stubborn slant to the bony jaw. His hair was dark brown, with a cowlick in its straightness unless he plastered it down, and in his immaculate white ducks and blue blazer he did not look much like a schooner captain. He looked more like the owner, which he was; at least he currently held title to the craft.

Actually, by virtue of a recent inheritance from an uncle he scarcely remembered, he was part owner, his partner being one of the local banks which held a sizable lien. This lien did not disturb him greatly, since he had never hoped to own a schooner of such size. Even so it had been one of his ambitions to cruise a boat of his own some day and for a young man who was about to realize that ambition he felt singularly dissatisfied without knowing why.

This mood had nothing to do with the schooner, which would presently earn him a neat profit. There was even a potential buyer lined up. If things went well the bank could be paid off and there would be a surplus to take back to New York when his leave of absence ended. The dissatisfaction, had he been able to analyze it, stemmed from a girl whose name was Sally Reeves. Sally bothered him when he allowed himself to think of her. To offset such inclinations he tried to keep his mind busy with other things. Now, hearing the hail from outside, he assumed it was the people he was expecting. Instead there was only this small bumboat from the Aquatic Club, a Negro resting on the oars while Howard Crane clung to the rigging and helped a woman to her feet.

"The others back yet?" Crane said, and then, not waiting for an answer: "All right to come aboard? I've brought a guest."

"Sure," Scott said. "Certainly."

The woman's grip was hot and moist as he helped her on deck, and she clung to his hand as Crane followed and made introductions.

"Julia, this is Alan Scott . . . Julia Parks."

"Lambert, darling," the woman said. "Julia Lambert, Mr. Scott . . . My," she said, "quite a boat we have."

The night was starlit but there was no moon and Scott could not tell much about Julia except that she wore a low-backed dress and carried a pocketbook. But he was aware that the smell of liquor on her breath was even stronger than the odor of perfume which enveloped her, that her voice was throaty and a little coarse, her accents American and suggestive of the city.

"Julia just flew in from New York," Crane said as they went below.

The woman did not seem to hear. She shook out her yellow-blond hair and glanced interestedly about the cabin, blinking a little against its brightness. When she had finished her inspection her glance came back to the well-stocked sideboard; then she looked right at Scott and smiled. "Howard thought we might get a drink," she said.

By that time Alan Scott was a mildly confused young man. And although he was not unduly imaginative nor given to the whispering of premonitions, he had one now as he made the drinks, and it was all bad. He was not sure why yet; he only knew that nothing must happen to spoil the ten-day charter he had arranged at three hundred dollars a day. With a two-man native crew and a party of five which did not demand deluxe service, he figured to clear better than two thousand dollars. The lockers were stocked, there were fresh fruit and vegetables aboard, a baked ham and a roast turkey in the icebox.

He had a chance to study the woman when she attacked her gin-and-tonic, aware now that she was somewhat drunk and likely to get more so. Her print dress with the square-cut neckline had style and she wore it well, but here where the light was good he saw that she was thirtyish and, though not tall, she had a voluptuous, full-blown figure that would one day be fat. Her eyes were heavy-lidded and expertly shadowed; her small mouth was vivid but there was a suggestion of petulant selfishness in the thin upper lip that cosmetics could not hide.

But what bothered him most was her name. Keith Lambert had recently inherited some two million dollars and in many ways he was the most important person taking the trip. It was because of him that the Farrows had arranged the charter.

"Is it—Mrs. Lambert?" he asked finally.

"Mrs. Keith Lambert."

Scott said, "Oh," and swallowed, the consternation growing in him and his blue eyes somber. "Oh," he said again. "I thought he was divorced."

"Not quite," Julia said, handing him her empty glass. "Not quite . . . Howard tells me you're taking a cruise."

Scott did not know what to say. He sensed that for some reason the woman intended to make trouble and he glanced at Crane, wondering how he happened to be involved. He understood that Crane was a native Barbadian—called "Bajans" on the island—who was one of the social elite and knew everyone. Right now he looked very natty in his white flannels, blue linen jacket, and knotted scarf, but it was at once apparent that he was not at ease.

His tanned, blunt-jawed face was grave and perspiring and his gray glance was concerned as he watched the woman. When he looked at Scott he seemed to understand the situation because he shrugged slightly, as though to say he was sorry about what was happening but helpless under the circumstances.

Scott turned back to fix Julia's drink. He handed it to her. He said yes. He said the Farrows had chartered the boat.

"The Farrows," Julia said. "Mark and Vivian. And my husband will be going, which will mean his chiseling little pal, Freddie Gardner will be tagging along. Anyone else I know?"

"A girl named Sally Reeves," Scott said. "She's Mrs. Farrow's step-sister."

Julia had moved forward to glance into the galley and down the alley-way beyond. Now she came back. She asked how many the *Griselda* could sleep.

"If you use these berths"—Scott gestured to indicate the main cabin—"ten."

"Ten. And only five are going?" Julia smiled, her veiled eyes busy. "Mmm," she said. "How cozy." She inspected her glass and then, without lifting her head, her glance came up. "In a way it's a shame."

Scott waited.

"I mean, wasting all that good space. Don't you think so, Howard?"

Crane took a silent but visible breath and said nothing.

Julia looked back at Scott and then, hearing a voice from outside, she said: "Maybe that's them now."

When Scott went topside Lambert and Freddie Gardner were already on deck and helping Sally Reeves aboard.

"Hi, Alan," she said in her friendly, American accents.

He said: "Hi," seeing now the oval of her face and the bright curve of her smile, but needing no moonlight to

know exactly how she looked. He had seen her constantly the past few days, often with his eyes closed at
night. It was nothing he wanted to do, for while that
part of him centering about the heart and stomach told
him he was in love with her the other part centering
in the brain reminded him that he was crazy, that Sally
had her eye on young Lambert and his money. Why
else, he asked himself, had she come down from the
States to take this cruise her sister planned.

"Someone else here?" Lambert asked when he had
sent the boat back for the Farrows.

"Howard Crane. And your wife," Scott said, keeping
his voice down.

Keith Lambert was a very tall and thin young man of
twenty-four with a somewhat unkempt look about him
that came not so much from untidy habits as from in-
difference. His straw-colored hair had a tendency to
slide across the corner of his forehead and he had the
slightly forlorn look of a college freshman about him
even when he was enjoying himself.

"What?" he said, and started to laugh. "Julia?" His
accent was British but not overwhelmingly so, and his
voice carried a tenor-like, immature cadence. "Oh, God,
no!" He peered down at Scott. "You're joking."

Scott said nothing while he gave Lambert time to di-
gest his announcement. It occurred to him that this
might make a difference in Sally's plans but he had no
time to dwell on the thought. For Freddie Gardner had
moved closer, a smallish, sandy-haired man of thirty or
so with a round, mobile face and glasses. In early times
he might have been a court jester, since he served in a
similar capacity for Lambert and stood ready to ap-
plaud all jokes when he was not telling his own. He had

a nervous way of laughing that, in a woman, would have been called a giggle. He did it now. He said:

"You can't mean it, Alan. Julia?" He turned to Lambert. "Well, at least she's only your ex-wife now."

"She says different," Scott said and followed them down the companionway into the cabin.

Julia had a half drink in her hand when she spotted Lambert. She tossed it off instantly, walked up and kissed him hard on the mouth.

"Hello, darling," she said. "Glad to see me?"

Lambert looked stunned. He wet his lips, as though tasting the lipstick and gin. He sat weakly down on the edge of the bunk, glanced bewilderedly about, then tried a smile.

"We're not still married, are we?" he said hopefully.

"But of course."

"But—you went to Reno."

"I know."

"I mean, I had some papers from there, a notice or something."

"You had a notice I was filing suit."

"But—"

Julia turned her back. She handed Scott her empty glass. "Do you mind?" she said.

Lambert tried again.

"But, really, Julia—"

"I went to Reno all right," the woman said, "but I didn't wait long enough. I had a chance to go to Hollywood. I went." She laughed boldly. "Wasn't I lucky, with you coming into all that money a month later."

She took the drink from Scott, tasted it, looked over at Gardner who stood wide-eyed and immobile, his jaw slack.

"And dear Freddie," she said, her thickening accents contemptuous. "Say something funny, Freddie!"

When Freddie remained momentarily tongue-tied with shock she glanced at Sally. "Hello, dear," she said. "You must be Miss Reeves."

Scott turned and fled, his face wet with perspiration and darkly scowling as his resentment mounted. The boat with the Farrows was just coming alongside and when they stepped aboard he told them what had happened.

For a long moment the two stood looking at each other, saying nothing at all, Vivian Farrow standing straight in her tailored dress and nearly as tall as her husband. Across the water from the direction of the Aquatic Club there came the sound of recorded music and somewhere along the beach in the direction of town there came, faintly, the beat of a native calypso band and a voice raised in song.

It was Mark Farrow who broke the spell. He had been sucking on his pipe, his head cocked as he listened to the conversation that came up through the open skylight; now he gestured with it, a note of regret in his well modulated voice.

"Well, I suppose we'll have to make the best of it."

"Nothing of the sort," Vivian said.

"You know how difficult she gets when she's potted."

"She's not the only one who can be difficult."

"But if she's still married to Keith—" He paused, tried again. "I mean to say, she could make things rather sticky for us if she wanted to. No use antagonizing her, is there?"

"She's not going to spoil our trip," Vivian said coldly. "Believe me."

3

SCOTT did not actually witness the meeting of the Farrows and Julia; instead he busied himself at the sideboard and tried not to listen. He made highballs for Gardner and Lambert, for the Farrows; he made a refill for Crane, who stood in one corner listening to everything and looking very much like a man who wished he were elsewhere. When he could he went on deck and sat down on the cabin-house near the skylight and put his head in his hands while his mind tried to shut out the voices below him.

Ever since he had left the Navy as the executive officer of an LST he had looked forward to the day when he could sail his own boat, preferably on some sort of deep-water cruise. He had known about his Uncle George, who had been knocking about the Antilles for years, even though the method of communication was a picture postcard once a year. He knew his uncle had a boat and he had thought there was a little money as well. What he had not realized was that the boat was an eighty-two foot schooner, not new nor having the interior finish of a Stateside-built craft, but sound and seaworthy nevertheless, with a workable diesel that would do five knots when pushed.

The attorney who had written him upon his uncle's death had given few details. On the strength of the letter Scott had managed a month's leave from the Madison Avenue advertising agency which employed him. He had arrived a week before to find that his uncle's estate comprised some second hand furniture in a rented bungalow, an almost vanished bank account, and the *Griselda*, on which the sum of $10,000 Barbadian was due the bank. Those who knew said the schooner might bring $15,000 at a forced sale, which was what Scott had in mind, provided he could cruise her before turning her in. At that point the Farrows solved one of the problems by offering to take a ten-day charter. It was the attorney who arranged it and Scott remembered the afternoon he had sat in the office overlooking Broad Street after the details of the estate had been covered.

"I don't know what your plans are for the *Griselda*," the man had said, "but if you'd like to charter her for a few days before you try to sell I have a party who might be interested. I think you could get a fair price. It might be quite profitable if you are so inclined."

Scott said he was interested and the attorney had immediately telephoned the Farrows, who said they would be right down. Scott had already been aboard the schooner and he had no doubt about his being able to handle her with the proper help. When he asked about this the attorney said that his Uncle George had managed quite well with two paid hands.

"He had a mate, who sailed these waters most of his life, and another native chap who served as cook and deckhand. Of course your uncle did much of the work himself."

"I'd expect to do the same," Scott said.

"Well, in that case I don't imagine you'd need anyone else. I think I could locate this pair for you and as I understand it Mr. Farrow would like to take a hand himself. He's done quite a bit of sailing."

Scott had been at once impressed with the Farrows.
Mark was a soft-voiced man with an unmistakable British accent and a straightforward manner. His wife was
dark-haired and handsome and her use of the vernacular told him at once that she was an American girl.

Once the introductions were over Farrow explained
what he had in mind. He said he knew the *Griselda* and
she was admirably suited for his purpose. What he proposed to do was to sail first to the island of St. Vincent,
then take a leisurely course down along the Grenadines
—Bequia, Union, Cannouan, Carriacou—stopping when-
ever the spirit moved them. They could spend a day
or so in Grenada, go from there to Trinidad and
then back to Barbados. He figured ten days would give
them plenty of time and he wanted to know what such
a charter might cost.

Because the proposition was unexpected Scott said
he had no idea. He said he'd have to think about it and
that the price would depend somewhat on the service
the Farrows expected.

"Not a great deal," Vivian said in her direct and un-
inhibited way. "We don't expect any hot and cold running maids or breakfast in bed. We can take care of our
own rooms if there's someone to do the cooking and the
dishes."

"You can count on me for a deckhand when you need
me," Farrow said. "Keith Lambert, too."

Scott liked these people and the idea excited him
quite apart from the prospect of the profit which might
be involved. He said he would let them know the following day and he spent that time in laying out an itinerary,
estimating the cost of the food which might be needed,

figuring when and where he'd have to use the engine
and the expense of the fuel.

There was no trouble about the crew. The mate, whose
name was Luther and whose antecedents were more
East Indian than Negro, had originally come from British Guiana. Luther had located the other hand. A Negro
Bajan of indeterminate age whose principal job with
Scott's uncle had been to serve as cook and steward, he
was eager to work again and the wages the two men demanded were relatively small. With this figure budgeted
along with other potential expenses, Scott gave Farrow
a price of three hundred a day, and was quite prepared
to knock fifty dollars from the price if necessary.

But Farrow had said yes without a moment's hesita-
tion, and a day later Keith Lambert solved Scott's other
problem, potentially at least, by saying that he might
buy the schooner if she acted well on the cruise. . . .

Now, glancing round as a shadow moved nearby, he
watched the shadow take shape and saw that it was
Sally. She sat down beside him without a word, folding
her hands and looking off across the starlit water at the
Aquatic Club pier, her very nearness bringing again the
unaccustomed fluttering in his stomach which had been
bothering him on and off the past few days.

Vivian Farrow had cabled Sally as soon as the charter
terms were accepted and Scott had seen her for the first
time when she came aboard three days later. She was
introduced as Vivian's sister, though the two looked
nothing alike, and Scott had been immediately impressed. He saw at once that her medium-brown hair
had glints of auburn in it, that her green eyes, framed
with long black lashes, looked right at you, not boldly
but forthrightly and with interest. A modern, independ-

ent, no nonsense girl was the way she seemed to him,
vital, friendly, curious. Only later when he saw her in
her swim suits did he realize how very nicely she was
put together.

She was easy to talk to and a common bond of interest
had been immediately established when he learned she
also worked for an advertising agency only four blocks
from his own—as fourth assistant copywriter on a cos-
metic account, was the way she put it. When he saw
she wore no wedding ring and understood she was to be
a member of the party he was greatly pleased, for, at
the time, he had assumed that this was to be simply a
pleasure cruise. Not until they took the *Griselda* out for
an afternoon sail the following day did he realize that
there was a more important reason for the cruise.

Keith Lambert had come along that time and Farrow
had a briefcase full of maps, plans, charts, and blue-
prints. Before the day was over Scott realized that the
Farrows were developing a resort island in the Bahamas.
They had, apparently, put all their money into the venture and had run out of credit. What they wanted from
Lambert was about a quarter of a million dollars—or any
part thereof—of additional capital. Scott also understood why Sally had been imported from the States.

Farrow had been at the wheel at the time, with
Lambert beside him. They had gone straight out from
the mooring to have a look at the flying-fish boats at
work and were on a reach to the leeward coast. The
crew was forward, the two women were below, and
Scott was sitting right where he was now, next to the
skylight, not eavesdropping but hearing a snatch or
two of conversation, mostly Vivian's, since hers was the
stronger voice. He never did hear Sally speak, but what

Vivian said was more than enough to give him the general idea of the younger woman's status.

"You don't have to sell anything to anybody," Vivian had said at one point. And again when the schooner rolled and the hiss of rushing water was momentarily stilled: "Actually all you have to do is be nice to him." And again: " . . . and what's wrong with marrying two million dollars?"

Since then Scott had tried to keep his emotional reactions in check. He had seen Sally almost daily but it was Lambert who was her most constant companion. They swam and rode and dined together, sometimes with the Farrows but often alone. When they came aboard Scott tried to remember that he was a hired captain and not a member of the party. . . .

A shout of laughter that was raucous, drunken, and unmistakably Julia's shattered such thoughts and he heard her say:

"You're not going to buy any island, toots, or build any club for Freddie until you've taken care of me."

Beside him Sally shivered. "How awful for Keith," she said.

"How awful for everybody."

"If there was only something we could do."

"We could give her a Mickey," he said, "if we had the Mickey."

Then, before Sally could reply, Julia's voice rose once more.

"What I want to know," she said, "is which cabin is mine? Where's that cute captain . . . Hey, captain!"

Scott moved swiftly, stepping past Sally and ducking below. Julia was sitting on the edge of the bunk, weaving a bit, peering slit-eyed at Vivian Farrow and Vivian was answering her, a straight-standing, high-breasted woman with jet-black hair and an olive skin that was now pale at the cheekbone. A one-time New York show girl, she had developed over the years a certain poise and self-assurance that sometimes bordered on the arrogant. She was that way now as she eyed Julia and tapped the tip of her cigarette holder between her teeth.

"There'll be no cabin for you, Julia," she said, her voice stiff and her American accent showing. "Not on this cruise."

"Ahh—" said Julia.

Farrow cleared his throat, a ruggedly built, pipe-smoking Englishman in his late thirties, with close-cropped dark hair and a sportsman's look. Now there were angry glints in his eyes but his voice was oddly calm and contained.

"She's quite right, you know."

"Nuts," said Julia.

"It's quite impossible, really. I mean, there simply isn't room, Julia."

"Nuts," said Julia again. "There's always room for one more."

"Not this time," Vivian said.

"In any case," Farrow said, trying his best to avoid an open argument, "it's nothing we have to decide tonight."

"Oh, yes it is."

"It most certainly is," Vivian said. "We chartered this boat and we're paying for it, and we'll say who'll go and who won't."

"Okay." Julia tried to straighten up and failed. "But get this. If I don't go, neither does Keith. How do you like that?"

For a long moment then the silence closed down on

the hot, smoky cabin, and for the first time Scott understood clearly just how much trouble this one uninvited
guest could make, how ruinous her presence was to the
plans and affairs of the others.

He glanced first at Howard Crane, blaming him somehow for what had happened even though he sensed that
he was being unfair in doing so. If Julia had been insist-
ent, Crane could hardly have prevented her from coming aboard. It seemed unlikely that Julia could make
trouble for Crane, now that his wife was away, but
right now he was a very unhappy looking man as he
stood there, his glance disgusted as it fastened on the
drunken woman.

He thought next of himself, and the charter on which
he had counted so much, of the preparations he had
made. He could not imagine a ten-day cruise with Julia
along; at least he could not imagine the Farrows sponsor-
ing such a cruise. Should the cruise be canceled, and
that's the way it looked now, he felt sure the Farrows
would reimburse him for any expense he had con-
tracted. What bothered him most was the thought that
if the charter was called off he might well lose out on
the sale of the schooner to Lambert.

He glanced across to the opposite berth where the tall
young man sat next to Freddie Gardner, aware that
Lambert's problems were more discouraging than his
own. Lambert, who was in love with Sally, now had to
contend not only with a wife who was out to make
trouble but who also seemed determined to make him
pay exorbitantly for his future freedom.

Freddie Gardner seemed also to realize what Julia's
presence meant to him. He sat very still in his white
drill suit, wrinkled now and frayed at the cuffs, his

round face moist and distressed. As long as he could
be jester and man-Friday to Lambert he had a liveli-
hood of sorts, for there were commissions to be made
from those who dealt, or wished to deal, with Lambert,
advances to be had, small payments for favors of one
sort or another, as befitted a pensioner for long and faith-
ful service. With Julia's dislike for him so evident such
favors would come to a sudden end.

As for the Farrows, it was easy to see why they were
so bitter. Julia's unexpected appearance seemed now to
be downright disastrous to their plans. From all ac-
counts everything they had had been invested in their
island venture and it was imperative that they raise additional capital, and soon. Until now it seemed to Scott
that Lambert was favorably impressed with their plans
and seemed likely to join them. But with Julia on his
neck haranguing and tormenting him the Farrows might
not get the chance to press their case. To them the cruise
meant everything and now . . .

It was Lambert who broke the silence. He cleared his
throat and straightened his thin shoulders. Looking
more than ever like an unhappy freshman, he brushed
the lock of blond hair back from his forehead and
made his final attempt, his voice thin, high-pitched, and
not very convincing.

"Please, Julia," he said. "Let's drop it for tonight, shall
we? Sleep on it and then in the morning we can discuss
things and see—"

"No." Julia peered at him glassily, her head rolling.
"We'll decide right now. If you go, so do I. That's exactly how it's going to be."

She reached forward to put her empty glass on the
table, missed, grabbed at it, and silently toppled for-

ward on her hands and knees, head down and blond hair obscuring her face.

For a moment then there was a taut silence, broken only by the sound of the glass as it rolled across the floor. Crane stooped and picked it up and they stood there like that while Julia pushed herself to a sitting position, head lolling.

Keith Lambert sighed audibly. "I'm sorry," he said to the room at large. "I'm afraid we'll never get her ashore now. Couldn't we"—he looked appealingly at Scott—"I mean, couldn't we put her in some cabin, just for the night?"

Vivian bit her lip. "She can sit there and rot for all I care," she said furiously.

Crane started slowly forward but Scott cut ahead of him to bend down and pick up Julia's limp form. He said the forward cabin was empty and now Sally stepped up, her young face distressed and her eyes understanding.

"I'll help you, Alan," she said.

They went forward, past the galley and round the jog in the passageway, past the double stateroom, the shower and head and the cabin opposite, coming finally to the one at the end. Sally stepped ahead to open the door and now Julia began to mumble, protesting that she could walk, demanding that she be put down.

Scott sat her on the edge of the bed and knelt to slip off her shoes while Sally worked on the zipper of the dress. She was still struggling when he backed out and closed the door, telling her he would wait. Apparently Sally had her troubles because even when he moved down the passageway he could hear her talking, and Julia's voice raised in argument. This went on for well over a minute and when Sally finally came out her face was flushed from exertion but the cabin was quiet. She was rubbing one wrist, her green eyes closer to anger than he had ever seen them when he thanked her for her help.

"I got her dress off and made her lie down," she said. "She'll be all right—I guess."

"At least she's quiet."

"That's because I put a pillow over her face."

Gardner had come into the alley-way to meet them and now he asked if Julia had passed out. When they said yes, he sighed and said, "Well, thank God for that."

Howard Crane was apologizing when they got back to the main cabin. He had a cablegram in his hand and was explaining how Julia had wired him from San Juan, asking him to meet her plane. He had taken her to the hotel where they'd had a few drinks and dinner.

"I happened to mention the cruise and after that, well"—he shrugged—"nothing would do but she come and have a look." He made a gesture of embarrassment. "I'm sorry. It was my fault."

"No." Lambert sighed heavily. "If she's right about still being married to me it wouldn't have made any difference. When she gets like that there isn't anything anyone can do."

"It's still my fault," Crane said, and suddenly he grinned. "Why not let me make amends? Couldn't we continue this somewhere else, for a drink at least? Morgan's perhaps, or the Flamboyant? We could salvage something of the evening."

He hesitated hopefully but the suggestion was received with lethargy rather than enthusiasm as one after the other demurred.

"Some other time, Howard," Farrow said. "For now let's just forget it." He glanced at his wife. "It'll be all right, dear. We'll get her off in the morning."

"It would be simpler," Vivian said, "if someone would conveniently strangle her."

"Maybe someone will," Freddie Gardner said and then, as though aware of the implication, he giggled.

Crane was already moving towards the companionway. He asked who wanted to go to the Aquatic Club and Lambert said they did, indicating Sally, Freddie and himself. Scott said he could put the Farrows ashore in the dinghy and there was no further conversation until he rowed them to the Yacht Club beach.

"Julia'll be all right, won't she?" Farrow said as he helped his wife out. "I mean you don't mind, do you, Alan, her staying aboard tonight?"

Scott said not to worry about it; he said Julia would probably stay dead to the world until morning.

"We'll be along then," Farrow said. "We'll get her off one way or another."

"And when we do," Vivian said, "we'll Shanghai Keith if we have to. Julia has fouled things up all she's going to. . . ."

The *Griselda's* main cabin was hot, stuffy and smoke-filled when Scott went below and, having had nothing at all to drink since dinner, the first thing he did was pour two inches of whisky into a glass and toss it down. He poured another quickly, added ice and soda and then got to work, first giving the carpets a quick sweeping and then collecting glasses and bottles. With the cabin in reasonable order he rinsed the glasses and then, abruptly, he stopped. For another moment he stood there, his cowlick showing, his blue gaze morose and brooding like his thoughts; then he chucked the towel away, finished his drink and strode back to the cabin, knowing that he had to get away for a while.

It did not matter where he went so long as it was away from the schooner, from the drunken woman in the forward cabin. What he needed was time for his mind to clear, a chance to let his ever-mounting resentment evaporate. When he had slipped on his jacket and turned off all the lights except the one in the galley, he went topside and climbed down into the dinghy.

4

THE CLUB MORGAN was well out in the country, per-haps three miles from Bridgetown, a low coral-stone building with a small bar, a good dance floor and an attractive, airy atmosphere. The orchestra usually played until three in the morning and because the club stayed open as long as there were customers it was the one place in Barbados where people could gather when the hotel bars had closed.

There were about a dozen cars parked outside when Scott arrived at twenty minutes of twelve. He had been there twice for dinner since coming to the island, and as he stopped to chat with Abe, the greeter and headwaiter, Howard Crane came into the foyer from the bar.

"Hello," he said, his grin rueful. "It looks like you and I are the only ones who reconsidered my suggestion."

Scott grinned back at him. "I had to get away from

there for a while," he said. "How about a quick one for the road?"

Crane shook his head. He said he'd had it. "I'm afraid I started much too early with you know who."

When he turned away, Scott went inside and sat down on a bar stool, ordering a double whisky and soda. As he waited for the drink he turned to look down at the dance floor and the half dozen couples who were performing for the six-piece orchestra, and now Frank Morgan, who ran the club with his wife Helen, strolled over and shook hands. Scott asked what he'd have and Morgan said:

"The same as you, only the first one's on the house."

They said: "Cheers," and then Morgan was asking about the cruise and saying it was a trip he wished he could take. He liked sailing and knew the *Griselda* well, but she was a little too much boat for him personally.

Scott listened morosely, not interrupting until Morgan had finished. Then he said he wasn't so sure about the cruise after all.

"Mrs. Lambert showed up tonight."

"Julia?" Morgan stared at him. "Here?"

"On this afternoon's plane."

"But—I thought Keith was divorced."

"So did he. She says no. She came aboard and raised hell with everyone. Didn't Crane tell you?"

"I didn't talk to him. He wasn't here very long and he wasn't looking too happy."

Scott said there was a good reason for Crane's attitude but before he continued he thought a moment about Frank Morgan. Morgan was an American from Connecticut who had come down here years ago and, with his wife, had started a small nightclub. When he could he

rented a larger place and finally had come out here in
the country and built this place which many said was
one of the nicest clubs south of San Juan. The local
news and gossip came quickly to a man like Morgan and
Scott decided there could be no harm in telling him
what had happened; besides, he wanted someone to talk
to, someone who was not involved.

It was part of Morgan's job to listen and he did so
now while Scott gave a brief but vivid version of the
scene, his tone glum like his thoughts, his gaze on his
glass. Now and then Morgan made some expression of
inarticulate surprise, mostly profane, and when the story
was finished he turned to a man who was drinking by
himself at the curve of the bar.

"Tom," he said, and beckoned. "Bring your glass . . .
Tom Waldron—Alan Scott."

Morgan waited until they had shaken hands and then
he said: "A friend of yours got in town today, Tom."

"Yeah?"

"Julia."

Waldron's face showed very little in the way of reaction. He eyed Morgan quizzically a moment, glanced
at Scott. In his mind there seemed to be but one Julia,
for he did not ask for further identification.

"Well, what do you know," he said. "I thought she
was through with the place. What brought her back?"

"Money, I guess."

Morgan went on to give the other a quick résumé of
what Scott had just told him. While Waldron listened,
head tipped slightly and his right hand using the bottom
of his glass to make wet designs on the bar, Scott took
the opportunity to study him, knowing right off that he
was American. The accent of a big city which colored

his words could be easily identified by anyone who had heard it before in the Bronx or Brooklyn. It took an ear, for Waldron seemed to have taken pains to disguise that accent, but now and then the slang came through.

Scott noticed first that he was quite clothes conscious. His slacks were blue, his jacket a white tropical worsted with the kind of lapels the local tailors incorporated in their work; his shirt was navy and his tie a yellow foulard. His hair was dark brown and thin on top, his ears large but close-set, his face, decorated by a mustache, seemed a little long in the jaw. He was not a large man but he looked fit, and behind his dark-rimmed glasses his eyes were deep-set and steady.

"I'm surprised she didn't show here," he said finally.

"She may have had it in mind"—Morgan grinned—"but she didn't make it. Right now she's sleeping it off in the forward cabin of the *Griselda*."

"Passed out?"

"Cold . . . Oh, excuse me—"

Morgan turned away to speak to a couple who were leaving. Waldron glanced up and then gave his attention to his glass which was now empty. When he spoke his voice had a remoteness in its connotation that suggested he was talking more to himself than to Scott.

"Quite a woman, Julia. Crane and I used to take her around some last summer after her husband had moved out." He paused to take a small breath. "She could be a lot of fun when she put her mind to it. She never pretended much and you didn't have to pretend with her. What you tried to do was not let her drink too much when she was out."

His glance came up, met Scott's and he pushed the glass aside with his fingertips. "I don't know why Lambert married her in the first place. She conned him into it, I guess. Because if you were with her enough and saw how she was when she'd been drinking too much you knew why a kid like him couldn't handle her . . . And speaking of the devil—" He turned away with a wink. "See you," he said.

Scott watched him move into the foyer, not understanding until he glanced round to find Lambert blinking at him, his thin face flushed and his straw-colored hair tousled and unruly.

"Hoped I'd find someone here," he said in his high-pitched voice. "Started home after I'd left Sally off and then couldn't face it alone. Decided I might as well get really boiled as the way I was."

"What happened to Freddie?"

"Oh, he toddled off to get his car while I was saying good night to Sally. Had it parked at the Yacht Club. Don't know what happened to him."

He called for another round of drinks, insisting when Scott tried to refuse, and then began to talk about what he called, "—that ghastly business on the *Griselda*." What he had to say called for little comment and Scott merely nodded agreement from time to time while part of his mind reviewed what he knew about Lambert, which wasn't much.

Lambert had come out from England four years previously, though no one seemed to know exactly why. He had a small but regular income and apparently the only constructive thing he had ever done prior to his marriage was to work for a while as a piano player at one of the local clubs. In many ways he seemed young even for twenty-four and his recent inheritance had done little to increase his sense of responsibility. He went everywhere, drank too much, often genially, although occasionally the end result was a fight of some sort.

Now, glancing out of the corner of his eye, Scott saw his companion weaving on the bar stool and knew he had already had too much to drink. He himself had come here with the same idea in mind but it was not working out that way. Instead of erasing his cares the liquor had served only to depress him; all he could think of was the charter and what would happen if the Farrows called it off or if Lambert decided not to buy the *Griselda*.

"Come on," he said abruptly. "Drink up and let's go home."

"Home?" Lambert eyed him blankly. He pushed the hair back from his forehead. "But it's early, man."

"Not so very. And we have to be on the ball in the morning."

"On the ball?"

"We have to get Julia ashore, don't we?"

"Oh, yes. Quite."

"We're still going to take the cruise aren't we?"

"Absolutely."

"I'll drive you home," Scott said. "I'll speak to Morgan. He can have your car sent over in the morning."

He found Morgan in the foyer and explained what he had in mind. Morgan said he would take care of it but when they walked up to Lambert he had already ordered a fresh drink.

"Appreciate it, old boy," he said to Morgan. "But not necessary, you know. Can send Freddie up in a taxi and he can pick it up. Might even do it myself."

He signed the check, said good night politely, and then went with Scott, staggering slightly but making no protest as he pointed out his car and stood by while the windows were rolled up and the doors locked. He accepted the key and seated himself with great care in Scott's rented Austin.

A narrow, bumpy road surfaced with crushed stone wound away from the parking lot past some native huts. They bounced along it for a fifth of a mile until they came to an intersecting hard-surfaced road, turning here past a tightly shuttered, unpainted shack that served during daylight hours as a neighborhood store. Then they were climbing a winding hill in second gear and, at the top of the plateau, driving past the row of tiny native cubicles which stood dark and stilted on either side of the narrow road, their windows and doors tightly closed against the night spirits. Not until they were rolling down Highway 6 did Lambert rouse himself and announce a change of plans.

"I'm going with you," he mumbled.

"Sure."

"I mean, I'm not going home. I'm going out to the boat."

"In the morning."

"Right now. Tonight." Then, before Scott could overcome his surprise, Lambert continued, his words thick and fumbling but his meaning clear.

"You don't know much about Julia," he said. "I do. Not everything, but a lot. Used to be a model. Worked in a dress shop and got to know quite a bit about the business. Came down from Miami on a holiday and decided to open a shop here. Don't want to bore you with my courtship but I was only twenty-two—she said she was twenty-five but she was closer to twenty-eight—and I'd never known anyone quite like her. Pretty when she wasn't drinking, a lot of fun but strenuous. I know why

I married her: fascinated. Never sure why she wanted me; think she thought I had money. Told her I didn't. Only a little income and no capital. No ambition. Told her so."

He paused, his breathing noisy and regular. He said: "Pretty exciting at first. Flattering to have a good-looking woman making a fuss over you. I tried to help out in the shop. Had big ideas about this and that but it didn't work out. Didn't know why until I realized Julia was dominating me. Had too much of everything. What I mean is, I couldn't cope with her. I was the husband but she was the head of the house. That sort of thing. She did all the thinking, made all the decisions. Fine so long as I agreed; when I didn't there was a battle. Trouble was she always won and finally, last summer, I had my fill.

"Moved out," he said. "Freddie and I set up bachelor hall. Stopped going to parties because I always seemed to run into Julia and another argument. Howard Crane took her sometimes; sometimes another chap named Waldron. Countryman of yours. From New York. Never quite understood him or just what he expected to find here. Retired, though he seemed young for that; said the climate was good for his health. Understood Howard better. Older. Around forty and knew how to handle women and his wife was in England for the summer. You don't know her. Very pretty, lovely girl. Only twenty-nine. Wealthy too. Lets Howard handle the money and invest in this and that and. . ."

His voice trailed off to end the monologue. His head tipped forward and then rolled slightly as Scott hit a curve and began to skirt the open, tree-bordered expanse of the Savannah.

Over on the opposite side and vaguely outlined
against the night sky was the grandstand, for it was here
that the local racing took place three times a year. At
other times it was a place for nursemaids, their carriages
and their charges, though on Saturdays or Sundays they
had to share it with the cricket match which seemed always to be in progress. For this was an island-wide sport
that ranged from the professional to what, in the States,
would be called sand-lot teams.

Obeying the stop sign as he came to the main highway, he turned right past the old fort overlooking Carlyle Bay, modernized now in spots and serving as a
barracks and training ground for the local regiment. As
they started downgrade, Lambert's head jerked back
and his eyes opened. Then, as though there had been
but an instant's interruption, he said:

"Where was I? Oh, yes. Well, by fall Julia decided
I'd told the truth about my income. Bored with me,
bored with Barbados. Said she'd get a divorce but
wanted money. I didn't have much but I had some jewelry my grandmother left me. Bracelets, some pins, a
ring or two. Julia said she'd take that, and she did. Went
to Reno. Very convenient for me but now she says there
isn't any divorce. So I'm going to talk to her. Tonight.
First time I ever had the courage and I'm not going to
waste the opportunity. Can't make you row me out but
I can swim it if I have to. Sorry to be sticky about it but
that's the way it has to be."

Scott tried to think of some answer as he slowed down
to approach the Yacht Club. The precaution was fortunate because as he swung round the curve he very nearly
collided with another car.

It was all over in two seconds and he was never sure

whether the car had been parked in the road with the lights off, or whether it had just turned out from the club. He saw the sudden glare of the headlights as the car angled in front of him and as he braked sharply he noticed that part of one lens was missing. As the car whipped past, gears grinding, he had the impression that it was an old model, and then it was gone and he was coasting in under the trees and cutting the motor, his thoughts reverting to the more important problem of his companion. He made one more attempt at persuasion.

"I don't blame you for wanting to tell her off," he said, "but it would be better if you waited until morning."

"I agree," Lambert said. "Much better. Unfortunately by morning I will no longer have this false courage I now possess. In the morning I will be my usual self: hungover, silent, spineless, a worm. No"—he opened the door and staggered out—"now is the time, old boy."

Rowing out in the dinghy Scott had one more thought predicated on the idea that in Lambert's present condition, another drink might finish him. He made the suggestion as soon as they were aboard. Why not, he asked, have one quiet drink before waking Julia.

Lambert examined him with half-closed eyes. He nodded and smiled crookedly. "Splendid," he said. "It will bolster my oozing courage."

When Scott returned with the drinks Lambert was leaning back on the starboard bunk, chin on chest and eyes closed. He opened them when Scott spoke to him, accepted the glass with thanks and took a swallow. Very carefully then he put the glass aside and closed his eyes again. A minute or so later he tipped slowly down on his side, lips parted and snoring faintly.

Scott sat where he was for a few seconds, then he took the two glasses and tiptoed into the galley, making no sound and feeling highly pleased with his strategy. When he came back he removed Lambert's oxfords, loosened his tie and carefully removed his jacket. He lifted his legs to straighten him out and that was when he saw the pocketbook.

It had slipped nearly out of sight between the cushions and as he retrieved it he recognized it as Julia's. For a moment or two he considered the woman but he had no intention of going to her cabin tonight. The whisky he'd had was working on him too and so he put the bag in a drawer of the sideboard, went to the galley to turn on the small, low-watt bulb there in case Lambert awoke and became confused in the unfamiliar darkness. Snapping off the overhead light he crept back through the cabin and along the deck to the forward hatch and down the ladder to his quarters. . . .

5

IN HER compact little Aquatic Club apartment—one of a row standing diagonally behind the Club itself—Sally Reeves sat huddled in the wicker chair by the window overlooking an angle of the sea. The Farrows had arranged for the apartment prior to her arrival because the spare upstairs rooms in their house were being painted. Later, when they were ready for her, Sally had become so pleased with the apartment and the feeling of privacy and independence it gave her that she had asked if they would mind too much if she stayed where she was. She spoke of its centralness and convenience. She said it would be much simpler for all concerned and although Vivian's reaction suggested the idea was pure nonsense, she did not argue when she saw Sally was in earnest.

Now, recalling that discussion, she understood that her decision had very nearly been a fatal one, and as her mind went on she realized that she was no longer quite so cold. The goose pimples that seemed for so long to have covered her whole body were mostly gone. Her breathing was even and regular once more and when she slid her hand inside her robe she could feel the strong, unhurried beat of her heart.

The chill which had seized her so relentlessly came not from her swim, nor from the air, which was still and warm; the chill was born of fear which even now re- mained stark and vivid in her mind.

She did not know what time it was nor how long she had been sitting here fighting off that fear. She did not know just when she went swimming or how long it had been after Keith Lambert had said good night. What she had done then had been motivated by her sleepless- ness and as her mind went back she could remember getting ready for bed, and lying down, then staring wide-eyed in the darkness while she thought about Alan Scott and Keith and Julia and the nightmarish episode on the schooner.

At the time she did not speculate on what might hap- pen tomorrow. She did not know whether there would be a cruise or not and she did not care much except for the Farrows' sake. She understood now why Vivian had

cabled her. She recalled how it had been delivered to
her office and how surprised she had been. Even then
she had not questioned the request because she alone
knew how much she owed her step-sister. Vivian needed
help of some kind and had she, Sally, been unable to get
leave she would have resigned because this was the first
and only time that Vivian had ever asked a favor of her.

She knew now how important the island venture was
to the Farrows and how Keith Lambert's participation
was essential to the future success of the venture, but
she did not think about such things now; what she did
think about was Alan, because she had been thinking of
him rather constantly ever since she met him and wondering what had happened to change him so.

She had been oddly attracted to him from the very
first. She was not sure why. She had known handsomer
men, men who were, superficially at least, more charm-
ing. Perhaps it was because it was so obvious to her that
he was so strongly impressed. She could tell by the way
he looked at her, the way he smiled; by the reflection in
his blue eyes and the way she could glance up sometimes to find him watching her while pretending he was
otherwise occupied. They had their work in common,
the background of New York and advertising, and the
same things seemed to amuse them at the same time and
it was nice to have him near her. That was the way it
had been until the day they took the afternoon sail;
since then something had happened that she did not
understand. There was a strange politeness and reserve
in his solicitude and it seemed almost as if he tried to
avoid being alone with her.

Because such thoughts had left her wide awake she
rose suddenly and reached for her bathing suit, the rest-

lessness working on her as she tugged it on and found
her cap, robe, and a towel. Not bothering with slippers
she had gone along the gallery and down the stairs,
continuing up the beach in the starlit darkness.

The water, at first touch cold, was warmly refreshing
as she felt it cover her. Its startling clearness, a deep blue
in the daytime, seemed faintly phosphorescent now. It
had an almost sensuous quality and she swam straight
out for a minute or two before turning over on her back
to float and think how much nicer it would be had she
dared to leave her suit behind. It was when she rolled
over that she noticed the yellow glow showing dimly
through the *Griselda's* port lights. She wondered about
this, not knowing what time it was, and then, surprisingly, she saw the dinghy move out from the schooner's
shadow and start shoreward.

She watched it a moment, thinking it was Alan and
wondering why he should be going ashore at this hour.
Secretly pleased at the thought of surprising him she
swam diagonally to intercept the dinghy. When she was
about fifty feet away she stopped to tread water and
hailed it softly.

"Ahoy, the dinghy!" she called, and waved one arm.

Seconds later she saw one oar dig in and the bow come
round. There was hardly a sound as the little boat approached her and she waited happily until it was almost
upon her before kicking off to one side.

It was well that she did, for what happened then came
without warning. She never knew who the oarsman was.
Darkness clothed him and he did not rise, so that the
upward angle of her vision was blocked by the dinghy's
hull. She heard a thudding sound as one oar was
shipped and then she was staring in shocked incredu-

lity as the other oar was raised straight up above her head.

It may have been instinct that saved her; more likely it was luck. Still not believing her eyes she saw the oar start to descend and sensed that the blow was deliberate. Then, panic striking at her and closing her throat, she kicked hard again and tried to duck under.

Somehow she did duck. She felt the water close over her head as she thrashed with hands and feet. She heard the slap of the oar and felt it strike her shoulder, but somehow she was swimming and feeling no special pain and knowing that what she had felt was only the pressure of churning water as the oar blade had knifed past head and shoulder.

She went down, and down until, ten feet below the surface, she felt the smooth hard sand beneath her fingers. Working along this and hoping she was heading towards the pier, she came suddenly to something hard and snakelike and slimy that angled upward immediately in front of her. She would have screamed had she been able to and the shock of her fear as her hand touched this thing was paralyzing in its intensity. Then, its very hardness telling her this was no animal, she knew it was the mooring chain of some boat and understood how it might be helpful.

Slowly, her lungs near bursting now, she let the chain guide her to the surface. When she felt the small buoy above her she grabbed it and, hoping to use the buoy as a screen, let her head slip carefully alongside with only her face above water.

The dinghy was fifty feet distant now and it was probably the slight phosphorescence in the water that gave her away. For even as she focused on the shadowy oarsman, she saw the blades dip and the bow swing swiftly towards her. With that she gulped air and, with no further attempt at stealth, dived again.

This time she knew where she was going. One glance had told her the black and spindly silhouette of the club pier was no more than fifty yards ahead of her, and now she swam diagonally towards it, still hugging the bottom. When she was forced to surface again the pier was closer and, still not glancing back, she launched into a furious crawl, not bothering to breathe until she slid between two protecting piles to safety.

For a while then she had no strength to swim, but lay on her back, floating and gasping for breath. She saw nothing more of the dinghy, heard nothing but the pounding of her heart. When she could she paddled under the pier to the beach beyond. Her knees were wobbly when she tried to stand but she forced herself to walk, instinct rather than conscious thought guiding her steps, the shock of her fear too great even to wonder about why such a thing had happened.

Even now, sitting here in the chair, she had no answer. She could not understand why anyone would want to kill her. She understood that some such idea must have been behind the attempt but it made no sense. The only thing she kept telling herself over and over was that the oarsman could not have been Alan. . . .

Mark Farrow turned uneasily on his bed and listened to the sounds of the party across the street. It had been going full blast when he and Vivian had come home some time before midnight, but it seemed now to be breaking up and he wondered how long he had been asleep, if at all. He did not remember dropping off, but then one never did.

Driving home from the schooner he had been unable to think of anything except Julia Lambert's arrival and her probable effect on the island venture in the Bahamas. Only he and Vivian knew how tenuous their credit position was and how desperately they needed fresh capital. Without it they stood to lose their investment and it was difficult to speculate just how much of Julia's former influence over her husband remained and what could be done about it.

It had been Vivian who had taken his mind off his immediate troubles and she had done it effortlessly and without conscious thought. She had done it simply by sitting there on the vanity bench and combing out her hair. The things she had to say about Julia and their problem were the same things which had been uppermost in his mind, but as he watched her he began to think instead of his wife and how different this marriage was from his first one.

He had stood in the doorway in his pajamas, his gaze speculating while she sat there unconscious of his inspection, nude except for the briefest of panties. It occurred to him then that her anger became her, adding somehow to the luster and color of her skin, and as he considered the line of thigh and breast and throat the idea came to him that sometime soon he must have a likeness of her just that way. Perhaps not a painting, since one could hardly hang it for others to see. But a piece of sculpture would be different. Something in wood like that fellow in Nassau did so well, dark rich wood with a high polish and shaped to duplicate her figure, say from knee to neck in the classic form.

He wondered if she would pose for such a thing and thought she would if she knew it would please him. Such a piece, headless if necessary, would preserve in replica the loveliness of her body against the future when they were older, and now, lying there in the darkness this thought came back to him, warming him anew. Such speculation was pleasant to contemplate but he could not sustain it in his new wakefulness. For presently, and in spite of himself, his mind again strayed to more pressing problems and he began to think about how he could stop Julia and what the following day might bring.

Right now he did not know. But Vivian might know what to do; she so often did when things seemed hopeless. Actually this island developing scheme was her idea, not his. During those first months of marriage they had discovered that between them their resources amounted to the equivalent of about $200,000. Invested at four per cent they would have $8,000 a year and here in Barbados, or in fact any of the islands, one could do quite handsomely, the exchange being what it was.

This, however, had not been enough for Vivian. She had ideas and ambition and the courage to take a gamble, once the odds seemed right. When she had learned the island was for sale she was at once full of plans for the future, and she went to those who could help her for the development of those plans. Things had gone well. They had a splendid start. Others had become interested, though not to the point of providing the needed capital.

But Vivian was a determined woman, in her love and in her loyalty. She was not one to give up easily. She would battle Julia right down to the wire, battle Keith Lambert too until convinced her cause was hopeless.

Somehow, some way, they had to get Lambert's financial support, and now, on impulse, he stood up in the darkness to glance out the window which overlooked the backyard and the house across the street where the party was starting to break up.

Quietly then, he moved to the open door of the dressing alcove connecting their rooms, crossing barefooted through this to the room beyond, having no thought of waking his wife but moved by some unknown compulsion to look at her again as she lay sleeping. Reflected light from outside filtered through the two open windows. He found he could distinguish the pieces of furniture and the white outline of the bed, and it was only when he had moved closer that he realized the sheet had been pulled down, that the bed was empty.

Across the street in the rear a couple said good-bye to the hosts of the evening, their muted voices sounding in the night air. A car door slammed and a motor started; not until it had accelerated and faded away in the distance did Farrow move. Then he leaned over the bed, feeling the pillows to make sure his eyes did not deceive him. Slowly, wonderingly, he straightened and peered about the empty room.

After a moment he walked to the front windows which overlooked the roof of the veranda and the beach beyond. He could hear, clearly now, the crunch and slap and hiss of the surf as it broke and rolled across the sand. He could see the white line where the curling waves started to break, the pale froth racing shoreward to die in the sand.

Unable yet to accept the fact that his wife was not here he stood motionless by the window until an explanation came to him. She had gone downstairs to get something to eat or something cold from the refrigerator. This is what he told himself and yet when he went to the head of the stairs and saw no light below he understood that this could not be. He went along the hall to the back window and only when he looked out at the open door of the garage and found it empty could he accept the fact that Vivian had left the house. . . .

Alan Scott was not sure what woke him nor did he know at first how long he had been asleep. He only knew that his eyes were open and staring at the overhead and he did not know why. For a few seconds he lay that way, wondering about it, conscious of the hot stillness about him, aware that his mouth was thick and his head was throbbing. When a glance at the radium dial of his watch told him it was only five minutes after two he sat up and began to curse softly.

One hour's sleep and here he was, wide awake. Why? With what he'd had to drink a man was entitled to sleep until morning; he'd heard no sound, was conscious of no movement and yet—

Prompted by some pressure he did not understand he stood up and climbed to the deck, clad only in shorts and feeling the welcome coolness of the night air on his moist skin. Aft, the schooner lay quiet and motionless like the water below. Overhead the sky was still black and starlit and all about the hulls of other craft were motionless silhouettes riding at their moorings. The Aquatic Club pier stood squat and dark against the shadows of the trees lining the beach but directly inshore he thought something moved just above the water line. For another moment he peered at it, seeking some identification, but if there had been any movement it was now lost in the shadows beyond.

He felt the wet spot on the narrow deck as he made his way aft. It felt cool and damp under his bare foot and as he stepped back he could see the darkened stain. A short distance beyond the boarding ladder was another similar stain and now, aware that the hatch was open and perhaps inviting to a native prowler bent on ·petty larceny, he hurried below, his instincts aroused and nerves edgy.

The cabin, dimly outlined in the faint light from the galley, was quiet. Lambert's body had shifted its position but it lay still and Scott thought he could hear the other breathing. More confused than worried, but driven by some inner compulsion he could not explain, he continued to the galley. After a quick glance he stepped round the jog into the passageway leading forward. It was darker here, and when he came to the forward cabin he hesitated, conscious of the sand under one foot as he leaned close to the door and listened. All he could hear was the soft thudding of his heart and now, still motivated by the prodding of instinct, he opened the door.

It was a narrow cabin, the bunk less than three feet away, and even in the half-light he could make out, vaguely, the figure on the bed. The port-light was open but the room was hot and humid and absolutely still. It took him a moment to understand why. He started to close the door; then he stopped, breath held and listening hard.

Like that it hit him, the sudden realization that something was horribly wrong. The room was *too* still. There was no sound of breathing, not even his own.

Then, the panic rising swiftly in him, he reached for
the light switch, blinking against the sudden brilliance.
He stepped inside, the sand still under his bare foot;
then he was staring incredulously, not at the still form
clad in brassiere and panties, but at the pillow which
covered the face and head.

It was hard for Scott to remember exactly what he did
then or even what he felt. Somehow he had the pillow
in his hand, seeing instantly the odd color which suf-
fused the woman's throat and face and contrasted so
sharply with her yellow hair. Yet it was only after he had
sought frantically for a pulse beat and found none, only
when he was quite sure she was dead, that he thought
to reverse the pillow and see the reddish stains smearing
the whiteness, to understand that if they came from
lipstick they had been put there by force.

The shock of this conclusion held him where he was,
the pillow still in his hand. Unable yet to think clearly,
his incredulous gaze moved slowly over the tiny cabin,
the built-in locker, the drawer beneath the bunk. He
saw the dress that Sally had hung on the wall, the shoes
and stockings on the floor. Everything else seemed in
place and there was no sign of a struggle. The still small
figure bore no visible mark and there was nothing at all
beyond the color of the face and throat to suggest that
violence had been done.

Somehow he knew even then it must be murder but
he did not remember casting the pillow aside and snapping off the light and closing the door. By the time he
could begin to think he was standing in the lighted
galley, weak-kneed and shaking. Then, forcing himself
to consider the circumstances, he swallowed against the
sickness in his stomach and looked in at Lambert, who

lay long and thin and motionless on the bunk, not on
his back as Scott had left him an hour earlier but on one
side.

For a fleeting second the thought crossed his mind
that Lambert might have awakened, as he had, and gone
in to see his wife. Lambert had come for that purpose,
had been determined to have some sort of showdown
with Julia that very night. Scott had tricked him into
taking that last drink with the hope of quieting him until morning. Apparently he had succeeded—but had he?
Who could say with certainty how long a man had been
asleep except the man himself? And with sleep so easy
to simulate, any such statement was open to question.

It did not occur to Scott then that he himself might
be suspect, that there was a time when he was alone on
board with Julia and that women had been killed by
men before who, having too much to drink, killed
not with premeditation but to silence one who fought
against unwarranted advances. No such thought
crossed his mind because right then he could think only
of Sally and the remark she had made about quieting
Julia with a pillow.

Suppose Sally had held the pillow there too long, not
intentionally but in exasperation. Suppose . . .

"No," he said, half aloud, and cast the thought away.
He would have to tell Sally what had happened, to warn
her to say nothing to the police. *She didn't do it.* That
was what he kept telling himself even while part of his
mind admitted the possibility. But she must be warned.

What he did then was motivated by two things: the
confusion in his own mind and his thoughts of Sally.
Still physically sick and badly shocked by his discovery,

he was unable to think past the simple fact that if Sally had not killed Julia, someone else had.

Beyond that he had no idea until he remembered the pocketbook he had found and now he went to the side-board and opened the drawer. He unsnapped the clasp to glance inside. He did not make a thorough search but when he saw the keys, the chain of small ones and the larger, hotel room key, the idea came to him. He did not stop to think whether this was the smart thing to do, or even if it was logical; for the impulse to find out what he could before the police moved in came only partly out of his own wretched confusion and indecision. His chief concern, though he did not understand this clearly until later, was the girl.

He replaced the bag. When the drawer clicked shut he thought again of Lambert and wondered if he could be awake. He turned quickly but the only thing that moved was his own shadow which fell across the bunk and obscured the thin face. When he stepped closer he saw the lids were closed. The mouth was no longer open and Lambert's breathing was quieter now. He did not wonder about it then but turned and quickly left the cabin. . . .

6

SCOTT approached the Aquatic Club apartments by way of the beach, and now, climbing the outside stairs and moving along the open gallery to her room, he only hoped he could wake Sally without arousing her neighbors.

He knocked softly and waited, listening intently. He knocked again. The third knock was longer and when he stopped he thought he heard a stirring in the room beyond. Presently a voice answered on the other side of the panel.

"Yes . . . Who is it?"

"Alan," he whispered.

The latch clicked and the door opened a crack. He spoke into it, leaning close but still unable to see beyond it.

"Something's happened, Sally. It's about Julia. I've got to talk to you."

After a three-second pause she answered. "All right. Just a minute."

"Don't turn on the light," he cautioned. "I'll wait."

He stepped back to lean against the railing and his hand touched something wet. When he glanced down he discovered it was a bathing suit which had been stretched there to dry. Then, as the door opened wider, he tried to think how he could best express the things he had to say.

He stopped just inside the doorway, seeing now the pale oval of her face and aware that she wore a long, light-colored robe, that there was a ribbon about her hair. Then, because he could think of no other way, he told her about Julia and how he had found her.

"Listen to me," he said when she tried to interrupt. "You're not telling the police about the pillow. You understand?"

"The pillow?" she said bewilderedly.

"You told me you put a pillow over her face."

"Well—yes—"

"That's how she died."

"What?"

"She suffocated."

"Oh, no!" She spoke quickly, her voice stiff with shock. "No, I—"

"Yes," Scott said. "I'm almost sure of it."

Sally listened again to his explanation, hearing each word distinctly and with a mounting horror that served only to bewilder her more. She had not been to bed and if the knock had come a half hour earlier she would not even have opened the door, so vivid were her own fears.

But during that time she had been able to think, to understand that Alan could not have been the man with the oar, that he would have had no reason to be rowing *away* from the schooner at that hour. Now, understanding finally what had happened to Julia but not yet fully comprehending all the implications of her death, she saw that there might be some connection between the murder and the oarsman. But at the moment this seemed less important than the things Scott was saying. There would be time later to tell of her own experience; what mattered now was that she convince him that he was wrong about the pillow. She took a breath. She picked her words with care even as she fought her rising panic.

"But I only did it to quiet her," she said in a voice she could scarcely hear. "I didn't—hold it there."

Scott reached out and took her hands and they were cold and limp in his own. He squeezed them and gave them a quick hard shake. With that her head came up and her slender body straightened.

"I'm not afraid to tell the police," she said. "I didn't

do it. I couldn't have." She hesitated, traces of hysteria
in the cadence of her voice. "I'll tell them—"

"No, you won't!" Scott's hands slid up to her elbows
and he shook them again. "I haven't called the police.
Maybe I should have but I didn't. Julia's not going to be
found until morning and you don't know anything about
a pillow. They'll find out how she died and they'll know
it was murder. You know you didn't hold the pillow
there too long but how can you prove it to the police?
How long is too long? . . . No," he said. "That's why I
came. You put Julia to bed but you didn't touch the
pillow. I haven't been here tonight. You came here and
went to bed. You don't know a thing."

He had other things to say, most of them repetitive.
At no time would he allow himself to think she could be
guilty, even accidentally so. The trouble was there were
no facts to support such a belief, certainly none the
police would accept. He could not tell her any of this
but for the first time he understood clearly the impulse
which had prompted him to learn what he could, while
he could.

For the important thing now was that the murder investigation be pursued until the guilty person was
found. Only then could Sally ever be sure she was innocent.

He finally got her promise of silence.

"Good girl," he said and squeezed her hand. "Try to
sleep. Take a pill if you have one."

The Carib Hotel, which stood well back from the
road and was approached by a semi-circular drive, was
a three-storied, vine-covered building, with spacious
grounds and a wide veranda extending across the front

and partway down one side. It was here that much of the daily social activity took place, but at this hour it was deserted and in shadow as Scott drove past and then parked under a tree so he could approach, not from the front but from the service wing on the opposite side from the lawn.

When he stepped to the ground he waited a moment, surveying the approaches. He had no knowledge of the inner geography of this particular wing but he was afraid to enter through the lobby. There would probably be a night clerk or watchman on duty there and it was essential to his plan that he get in and out without being seen, at least until he had a chance to inspect Julia's room.

There was a light over the door which served this wing and when he saw no one about he started for it, keeping to the shadows as much as he could. The last fifty feet were in the open and he covered this distance at a normal gait, his face turned away from the light. Then he was inside and walking down a corridor that was hot and humid and filled with the smells of cooked food. Other doors opened from this corridor but there was only darkness beyond them and he kept on, turning now in a jog to the right and coming finally to a wider hallway which led from the lobby. Here carpeted stairs led upward and he met no one as he went along the second-floor hall to room 208 which overlooked the lawn. Because the light was bad he had a little trouble fitting the key in the lock but presently the door was open and he stepped inside, groping along the wall for a light switch as the door swung behind him.

What happened then came unexpectedly as the darkness closed in on him. He had been moving slowly, intent only on locating the switch, but now he stopped, his arm outstretched, the sharpest of sensations ripping along his nerves. He was for that second frozen in his track and he did not know why.

Moving only his head, he turned slowly, nerves still tingling as he tried to penetrate the darkness. When there was no sound or stir of movement he brushed off the intuitive warning, deliberately, telling himself the protective impulse was born of an imagination momentarily out of hand.

He took another step along the wall, still groping; then he sensed rather than heard the rush of movement beside him and knew too late that instinct had been right. Someone was in the room; someone had been waiting for him to take the step and even as he knew this an unseen blow clipped him on the side of the head and knocked him against the wall.

He tried to turn as he slid along it. He lashed out blindly with his right and missed. He staggered off balance and heard a quick grunt of exertion and then a fist smashed against his cheekbone.

This time he went down but at no time did he lose consciousness. He heard the scurry of feet and he swiveled on one knee, lunging in the general direction of the door in an effort to block it off. He came erect, bracing himself as best he could, left hand extended, his right cocked. Only then did he realize that the sound he heard was the rasp of window shutters across the room.

Even though he whirled in the directon of the sound it seemed to take him a long time to move. With anger replacing his surprise he lunged forward, seeing now the rectangle of the window but not seeing the chair that tripped him before he was halfway across the room.

He fell heavily and kicked the chair away. He got up. He stumbled against the bed, recovered his balance and continued towards the window. All this had taken no more than ten seconds. No word had been spoken. What noise there was had been made by his own clumsy efforts and when he came finally to the window he knew that he was alone in the room. When he looked down there was only the empty lawn bordered in shadows, and the wrist-thick vines matting the wall and telling him how the prowler had entered and escaped.

Leaning back inside the room he stood where he was, breathing hard and his resentment mounting, not so much at his unknown assailant as at his own carelessness. The side of his face was tender and one shin throbbed but he was otherwise unhurt. He knew he had been struck by a fist, which meant the intruder was a man, and he understood that it was surprise and the darkness which had made him such an easy victim.

Flame from his cigarette lighter disclosed a lamp on a table desk and when he had drawn the shutters he snapped it on; then he saw the three bags on the bed, two of which were open. The dresses in the largest of these were a tangled mess and he wondered if this had been opened by Julia on her arrival. The locks on the medium-sized bag had been forced and here too the contents had been partly scattered on the counterpane. The third and smallest bag was still locked, and as he took the key chain from his pocket he decided that either the prowler had been surprised before he could force it open, or that he had found what he wanted in the second bag and had been trapped before he could get away.

When Scott lifted the lid he saw that there was a smaller, leather case inside, which, when opened, dis-

closed an assortment of earrings and pins and bracelets.
There were some folded underthings, stockings, a writing kit, slippers, a robe. At the bottom was a long envelope which he opened. Unfolding the papers inside
he started to read; just as suddenly he stopped, staring
now at the wall as his head came up and he let his
breath out.

For what the papers officially proclaimed was that
Julia Lambert had been granted her divorce more than
three months ago. According to the terms of that divorce she had no further claim on Keith Lambert and
yet—

Scott replaced the papers and envelope with nervous
fingers. He could not help asking himself why Julia had
come here to attempt such a colossal bluff but he made
no attempt to find an explanation now. Too many other
questions were demanding answers and it occurred to
him that this was not the place to hold a one-man con-
ference.

He closed the small bag, locked it. He turned off the
light and left the room, taking time to lock the door
before hurrying downstairs. As before he was fortunate
in meeting no one but it was not until he was in his car
and on his way that he took time out to think.

The speculations and deductions that came to him
then were arrived at by a primer-like simplicity starting
from the known fact that the intruder in room 208 had
been a man, and his first reaction to this was one of elation because it seemed to prove that Sally Reeves had
not killed Julia. Only when he probed further did he
realize that such an assumption did not necessarily follow.

Everyone who had been aboard the *Griselda* knew

that Julia was spending the night there. They must, therefore, know that her hotel room would be empty and easy to search. That the search had been so long delayed was also easily explainable to anyone who knew the habits of the Carib's clientele. The broad veranda was seldom empty until one thirty or two in the morning, and without a key the window was the only way to reach the room, an impossible undertaking until the veranda was deserted.

"So what does it prove?" he asked himself aloud.

"Nothing," he said by way of answer, "except that someone killed Julia, and a man searched her room."

Reluctantly he admitted that the same person need not have done both. He did not know what the prowler wanted, nor could he speculate with any intelligence. The only other fact about which he could be sure was that the man in room 208 could not have been Keith Lambert—which left Mark Farrow, Howard Crane, and Freddie Gardner. . . .

It was nearly four o'clock when Scott returned to the *Griselda* and he did not bother to inspect the main cabin but went forward to his quarters and undressed. By now the weight of physical and mental exhaustion had begun to work on him but he had no intention of going to sleep. Having already postponed calling the police because of his desire to protect Sally, he had decided that his best course was to pretend he knew nothing about Julia. He would carry on as if nothing had happened, and at the proper time he would discover her body.

This was to be the day of the cruise and it would be logical to be up early, and so at five he put on his trunks and t-shirt and went on deck. For another half hour he sat there, watching the sky grow pink. Gradually the palms took shape along the beach, and in a little while the sun began to kiss the tops of the feathery casuarina trees which backed the palms in their march along the shore.

The flying-fish boats from a nearby beach settlement were already tacking seaward, and as he turned to watch them he saw the steamer coming in from the east, the colors of the Harrison Line on her stack, a cargo-passenger ship of modern design with a black hull and white superstructure. She seemed surprisingly close inshore as she angled in for an anchorage on her first stop since leaving Britain, and Scott watched the water churn white astern as her screw was reversed and she moved toward her berth close by an older, sister ship which had come up from the south the day before.

An angle of land obscured the inner reaches of Carlyle Bay and when the ship slid out of sight, he rose reluctantly and dived over the side for the morning swim that had become a part of his daily ritual. It was his idea to maintain the normal routine until the time came for a logical discovery of the dead woman so he took his time. When he was ready he toweled off lightly on deck and then put on some clothes.

Keith Lambert was snoring loudly when he went below to start the coffee, and with no effort to be quiet he started the generator. Lambert kept right on snoring and Scott waited until the coffee was nearly ready before he went over and shook his passenger awake.

"Hit the deck!" he said.

Lambert groaned. Scott shook him again, watching the lids open a fraction of an inch at a time until finally the bloodshot eyes began to focus. Almost immediately Lambert closed them again. He groaned. He wanted to know what time it was. When Scott told him he wrenched his skinny frame to a sitting position and, accompanied by more groaning, held his head.

"I feel horrible," he said.

"You're going to feel worse," Scott said, and then he told the news about Julia, speaking with a blunt incisiveness to relate the facts as he had rehearsed them. He said he had knocked at Julia's door when he came down to put on the coffee; when there was no answer he looked in. She was dead.

Lambert's first reaction seemed to be one of incredulity. His jaw sagged and he swallowed visibly. When he could speak he said he didn't believe it; he tried to argue until Scott told him to go look for himself. By that time Lambert's bloodshot eyes were sick and his thin face was gray. He staggered erect, blond hair standing on end. He rubbed the back of his hand across his lips. His high-pitched voice cracked when he replied.

"I—I couldn't . . . I think I'm going to be sick," he said and lurched from the cabin.

He still looked sick when he came back to the galley. "Good God, Alan," he said. "Who could have done such a thing? Are you sure?"

"Did you look?"

"I couldn't." He swallowed against his sickness, his face pasty. "I've got to have a drink," he said. "Something. Anything. . . Please!"

Scott said it would be better if he didn't. It would be a tough day. "Coffee would be better," he added. "With maybe some tomato juice."

"Yes. Tomato juice—but with a spot of gin, Alan. Please. And some worcestershire."

Scott fixed the juice and Lambert reached for it with

shaking hands. He drank greedily and then looked up.

"What about the police? Shouldn't we call them?"

"That's why I woke you," Scott said. "We don't want just anyone out here at first. Who do you know? Who's a good man to call?"

Lambert thought it over and it took quite awhile. Finally he sighed and said: "Major Briggs, I guess. He's the Deputy Commissioner."

Scott nodded. He said he'd row ashore and put in the call. He said if he were Lambert he would stay away from the bottle. . . .

When Scott pushed away in the dinghy he saw his two-man crew sitting on the beach waiting for him as was their custom. Until that moment he had forgotten all about them and now he changed course away from the Aquatic Club and headed for the beach.

They made an odd pair as they stood up at his approach. Luther—Scott did not know whether this was the man's first name or last—was thin and wiry, his light brown coloring of a shade that might have passed for sun-tan at someplace like Miami Beach. He was clad in well washed khaki trousers and shirt, and wore sneakers and an old felt hat. Such inquiries as Scott had made assured him that Luther was a fine hand with a boat and knew thoroughly the waters and ports from the Virgins to British Guiana. Luther's one reported weakness was an occasional overfondness for rum but as yet Scott had seen no evidence to support the opinion.

Boult was a bigger man, and quite black. His khakis were neatly patched and he was barefooted, but he was a clean-looking Negro with a soft deep voice and a thick "Bajan" accent that made him difficult to understand at times. The important thing to Scott was that Boult could cook and knew how to serve, and now he was a little worried as to just what he should say.

He did not rise as the dinghy grounded but spoke across the bow. He said that they would not be sailing today. He said plans had changed unexpectedly and it might be two or three days before they could start the cruise.

"I'll let you know when I want you," he said, "and you'll be paid whether you work or not."

They nodded but said nothing. As he started to back off the beach Boult stepped forward to give the boat a shove and they were still standing there as Scott began to row toward the Aquatic Club and a telephone. He was nearly to the pier landing when he noticed the native on the beach.

The man had been walking slowly along, poking at this and that with a long stick, and as Scott watched him, he stooped down and picked something up. Scott wasn't sure what it was but he saw there were two pieces and one looked like a towel. When the man glanced up and saw Scott watching him he tucked the things under his arm and started toward the shore end of the pier while Scott continued to the landing, giving no further thought to the incident until much later.

Major Briggs arrived in a Harbor Police launch forty minutes later along with a doctor, two uniformed constables and a Negro sergeant in plain-clothes. A stocky, competent-looking man of perhaps forty, he looked very neat and efficient in his khaki shorts, cap, and jacket. His Sam Browne belt was sleekly polished and he carried a swagger stick which he rapped against his stock-inged calf from time to time.

Pausing in the main cabin only long enough for the briefest of fill-ins, he continued to the forward cabin with the doctor while Scott and Lambert waited it out in silence. This lasted perhaps ten minutes and then the two constables appeared with a stretcher and blanket. With that, Lambert, who had bathed and shaved but still looked seedy, fled topside.

When the launch cast off leaving Briggs and the sergeant behind, Lambert came back and Briggs got down to business. He wanted to know what they could tell him, listening attentively as they explained what had happened at the party and nodding from time to time as the sergeant jotted facts in a notebook.

"And after you went ashore," Briggs said to Lambert, "you took Miss Reeves home. Freddie Gardner wandered off to his car. You started to drive home, changed your mind and went to Club Morgan. You had some drinks and came back here. Why?"

Lambert blinked. "Why what? I mean—"

"Why here instead of home?"

"I really can't say. I grant there must have been some reason but"—Lambert sighed and his shoulders sagged still more—"I can't seem to recall it. What I mean is, I had a bibful, Major. Don't recall coming aboard. Must have though, since I was here."

Briggs glanced at Scott, his brown eyes speculative. "Maybe you can tell us, Mr. Scott."

Scott hesitated, but not for long. To protect Sally he knew he had to lie but he saw no reason why he should lie for anyone else.

"Keith wanted to talk to his wife," he said.

"Oh?"

"Said he'd never had the courage to tell her off before."

"You agreed to this, knowing her condition?"

"It wasn't a question of agreeing. He said I could row him out or he would swim. So I brought him along and fed him another stiff drink, hoping he'd fall asleep and forget about his wife. Apparently he did. I took off his shoes and jacket and left him there on the bunk."

Briggs put his hands on his bare knees. He took time out to study Lambert. "Did you get up during the night?"

"No."

Briggs' smile was small and tight. "For a man who can't remember coming aboard, you seem quite positive . . . Well"—he rose and reached for his cap—"we'll need some statements. I'll get in touch with the others." He glanced at his watch. "Let's say ten o'clock if it's convenient. At my office . . . If you can put us ashore now," he said to Scott, "I should have a car waiting."

It was then, as Briggs started to go, that Scott remembered Julia's pocketbook. He spoke of it, explaining where he had found it as he took it from the drawer. Briggs inspected the contents, looked at the keys, straightened out a crumpled yellow sheet that Scott had not bothered to examine. When he read it Briggs' brows lifted; then, giving Scott a level glance, he replaced the contents. He thanked him. He said it might be important.

7

MAJOR BRIGGS' office was on the second floor of an old stone building, one of several that stood about a paved courtyard in downtown Bridgetown and formed the Central Police Station. Overlooking this court and the huge Indian evergreen in the center was a covered veranda with Demerara shutters. Two plain-clothes men and a policewoman worked here at desks and the tiny anteroom at the end was empty when Alan Scott arrived shortly before ten. He was admitted to the private office as soon as he gave his name, and what happened then surprised him a little.

The Major, pleasantly businesslike, waved him to a chair at the end of the desk. He pushed a pad of paper and a pen at Scott and leaned back in his chair. There was no cross-examination, threats, or insinuations. What Briggs wanted was a simple statement in writing as to what Scott knew about the affair.

"Just put down what you told me earlier," he said. "Plus anything else that may have occurred to you since then. Just the simple truth will do for now, Mr. Scott, though I do wish you'd give some thought to time."

"Time?"

"Perhaps I should have said the time element. When Mrs. Lambert was taken to the cabin, when the others left, things like that." He smiled faintly to indicate that he did not want to be unreasonable. "Not that I expect you to be exact. One doesn't go about looking at clocks at a time like that but—do the best you can."

Having already decided to stick to his story, Scott wrote it down, hardly expecting that this would be the end of the investigation but glad that there was to be no inquisition for the present. When he had finished, Briggs read the statement, called an aide in and had him witness Scott's signature.

"That'll do for now," he said. "Thank you very much." He rubbed his palms gently together, hesitated; then stood up. "I'm going to ask you to stand by for an hour or so, if you don't mind. Until I've talked to the others."

Scott frowned, the disappointment showing in his angular face. At the point of congratulating himself on the simplicity of the interview, he understood now that this was only the beginning.

"Here?" he said.

"Well, no." Briggs waved one hand. "We're hardly equipped to make you comfortable, but you might wait on the downstairs veranda, or in your car if you prefer. Just so we can find you when we want you."

Scott eyed him sardonically. "You mean you want to have another session with all of us after you've compared notes."

"It's sometimes helpful," Briggs said, and smiled pleasantly but with no great warmth.

Scott went out to find Sally and Lambert waiting in the anteroom along with Freddie Gardner. They all stood up and Briggs, who had followed Scott, was introduced to Sally.

"Should we come in now?" Lambert asked.

"Well—yes." Briggs smiled. "But one at a time, if you don't mind. Suppose we start with you?"

Lambert, looking like a man who wanted to protest but did not dare, glanced at Sally, shrugged and followed the Major. When the door closed, Scott took the girl's arm.

"We should have time for a cigarette," he said. "Will you excuse us, Freddie?"

Freddie wet his lips. He wore another of his white drill suits with raveled cuffs and this one had a stain on one pocket. His round face held a melancholy look and behind the spectacles his light brown eyes were distressed and uncertain.

"Yes, certainly," he said reluctantly, "although I do wish someone would tell me just what happened."

Sally wore a navy-blue linen dress and carried a straw bag. She was bare-legged and though her green eyes were subdued her tanned skin looked fresh and flawless and he liked the way she kept her chin up. But as they went down the stairs his mind held no thoughts of love. He was worried about how she would react to Briggs, and he was annoyed that she had come here with Lambert instead of him.

"You're all set, aren't you?" he asked when he gave her a cigarette and a light.

"I don't know."

"What do you mean you don't know?" That was what he wanted to say. He wanted to shout at her and shake her and make her see how important this was to her.

"Just remember you know nothing about anything," he said, concentrating on his voice. "After the party you went home and went to bed."

She turned as he spoke and put her hand on his arm, her gaze troubled and her brow furrowed.

"I'm not sure this is the right way, Alan. I have nothing to hide."

You've got plenty to hide! That's what Scott thought but he did not say so; he did not try to explain that if she told the truth about the pillow she would be a suspect, and might possibly always remain so. He forced a smile. He squeezed the hand on his arm. Then, seeing the Farrows drive up, he said:

"Play it my way. Forget the pillow."

With that she turned and went up the stairs and he waited for the others.

Mark was clad in white shorts and a sport shirt which contrasted sharply with his sunburned skin and dark hair. His squarish face was grave but his accented voice was as soft as ever as he said good morning.

"Have you finished already?" he asked.

"The first round."

"First round?"

"There'll be a more general inquisition later. I've been told to wait."

"Oh?"

"What, exactly do they want with us?" Vivian asked.

She stood tall and straight in her beige dress, her olive-skinned face impassive but impatience in her voice and a hint of nervousness lurking in the corners of her black eyes. She had a half-smoked cigarette between her fingers and she threw it away as she spoke. She shifted her bag under one arm, her glance straying to the floor above.

"Just a statement," Scott said. "For now."

"Like what?"

"Like what happened after the party. Where you went and—"

"We went home," she said, interrupting. "We stayed there."

"Which is what we tell the Major," Farrow said. "Suppose we get on with it . . . Oh," he said as an afterthought. "About the cruise."

"Yeah," Scott said.

"How would it do to meet us at Goddard's when we finish here? We could discuss it then."

Scott watched them enter the doorway. When they started up the stairs he sat down on the railing but before he had a chance to look about another car entered the narrow, tunnel-like entrance from the street. He watched the sedan back round and park at one side and then Howard Crane came along the court and up the steps.

"Good morning," he said. "Anyone else here?"

"Everyone's here."

"Everyone?"

"Everyone who was aboard last night."

"Oh. And what is one supposed to do?"

"Give a statement, I guess."

"About what? I mean, what is there to say?"

Scott said he guessed Briggs wanted to compare notes as to what had happened aboard the schooner and where people went afterward. Crane listened, a restlessness working on his flat-muscled body so that he was unable to remain still. His tanned face was grave and his gray gaze seemed worried. He said it was a shocking business; he could not understand how such a thing had happened unless it was just an unfortunate accident; even that was hard to accept.

He seemed to expect no answers to his comments and presently he was gone and Scott was looking off across the court to where a squad of uniformed constables was lined up in front of a sergeant. Apparently this was an inspection of some sort because the sergeant looked over each man's equipment in a precise and military manner before he marched them away.

Through the open doors and windows of the one-story frame building which made up two sides of the court other officers were busy with paper work, and there was a constant going and coming from the one two-story structure in the corner which apparently served as a barracks of some sort. Beyond this and to the right he could see through the trees the courthouse in the next block. Court—in the States it would have been Superior Court though he did not know the term used here—was in session. The *Daily Advocate* chronicled the facts of that court and Scott knew that at the moment a manslaughter case was being heard, a knifing of some sort involving two natives. Through the high open windows he could see the backs of the spectators, the white jackets of the constables acting as attendants; on the pavement outside little groups stood here and there beneath the mammoth evergreens.

Scott continued his idle inspection until Freddie Gardner came through the doorway and moved up beside him, removing his spectacles to mop his moist round face and then starting to polish the lenses. He accepted the cigarette Scott offered with thanks. He said he much preferred American cigarettes when he could get them.

"The trouble is," he said, "the only chance one has is to go aboard some of the ships that come in. Like the *Colombie* for instance. She'll be in this week. French. Very pleasant to go aboard for lunch if one is in funds. Best to take a woman. Handbags, you know. Need one

to stow your carton of cigarettes. Customs knows what's
going on of course but they won't bother you if you don't
make it obvious."

Sally and Lambert came out to join them shortly and
Scott could not tell by looking at her how it had gone
with Briggs. Little was said by anyone as they lined up
along the rail and presently the Farrows enlarged the
line. When, ten minutes later, a constable came to tell
them Major Briggs was ready, they filed in through the
door and up the stairs.

Chairs had been moved into Briggs' office and he remained standing until everyone had been seated. While
he busied himself with the statements on his desk, Scott
glanced round at the various charts which adorned the
walls. The one closest to him seemed to show the break-
down of the various districts and sub-stations that covered the island, the colored pins spotted here and there
to indicate the complement of officers and men. Across
the room another chart seemed to indicate a month-by-
month record of island crime in its various ramifications. Then Briggs was talking, still very pleasantly,
telling them how much he appreciated their cooperation.

Briggs was no amateur. He had been in the Colonial
Service for many years, as the crowns on his shoulders
indicated. He had served in Kenya and the Gold Coast
before being assigned to Barbados and would one day
move on to another station befitting his rank. He had a
habit of rubbing his palms gently together when his
mind was working and he did so now before he ad-
dressed himself to Sally, his tone conversational rather
than accusing.

"These statements give me a rather good picture of

what happened last night," he said, "even though we will have to await the police surgeon's report before we can be positive as to the cause of death. Right now I don't want to inconvenience any of you any more than I have to, so if you can help me clear up one or two details, Miss Reeves, this shouldn't take long."

Scott was watching the girl and he liked the way she looked at Briggs, the way she sat in the straight-backed chair. Erect and ladylike without being stiff, she had her feet flat on the floor, knees together and her hands at ease in her lap. She looked cool and composed in her navy dress and Scott was so busy liking what he saw he did not hear Briggs' opening remark. What he did hear, and it scared him, was the word Sally spoke.

"Pillow?" she said.

"Yes." Briggs indicated a sheet on his desk. "In your statement there is no mention of your using a pillow."

"Using—"

"You were overheard to say that you quieted Mrs. Lambert with a pillow, something to that effect."

Scott's face was suddenly tight and something froze inside as a strange and shapeless fear began to work on him. He stared at Sally, his eyes anguished. He watched the color ooze from her cheeks and her lips part, as though she had been struck a physical blow. For an instant her glance touched his and when he saw the tortured look in her eyes he knew what she was thinking: he had told her to say nothing about the pillow but someone had, and he was the only other one who knew about it. He wanted frantically to speak up and could not. He wanted to signal her in some mute way, to tell her she was wrong, to shake his head. He did

shake his head, scowling hard, but by that time Briggs
had continued and she did not see him.

"Is that what you said, Miss Reeves?"

"No." Sally shook her head and her voice was hardly
more than a whisper. "I mean, I may have said something like that but I didn't—not really, that is—"

"You didn't use the pillow?" Briggs prompted.

"Well, there was a pillow and I did pick it up and—"

"And because she was noisy you put it over her face
and held it there?"

Scott could only watch the girl, an agony of despair
warping his thoughts as he sought some way to help
her. Somewhere in the room there was a murmur of denial, the sound of a breath sharply drawn. Then someone spoke, bluntly and with force.

"Just a moment."

Scott saw that it was Mark Farrow. He had leaned
forward, his squarish face dark and scowling.

"Isn't that rather putting words in Miss Reeves'
mouth, Major? Shouldn't she be allowed to say what she
has to say in her own way?"

Briggs considered the question. He rubbed his palms.
He nodded. "I wish she would," he said without animosity. "Mr. Scott carried the woman to the cabin," he said
to Sally. "You partially undressed her and she stretched
out on the berth. Did she protest?"

"Well, yes. In a way. She swore at me."

"Then what?"

"I turned out the light and when she tried to sit up
I pushed her back. There was an extra pillow—"

The sentence dangled as she faltered and her glance
dropped before the Major's steady gaze. He prompted
her again.

"You put it over her face?"

"It was more—well, I suppose I did. I *tossed* it over her face."

"You didn't press down on it?"

"No," she whispered and then, more firmly as her chin came up: "No."

"Do you know what effect that had on her? Did she struggle or try to throw the pillow aside?"

"I don't know," Sally said. "I didn't stay to watch. I went out and closed the door."

"Very good," Briggs said. "I think that's clear enough for the present." He shuffled the papers on his desk and then glanced up, his gaze touching each of the others in turn. "There's just one other point that could stand some clarifying and I'm afraid this also has to do with you, Miss Reeves."

Talking to the room at large, he said: "As most of you know there's quite a bit of what one might call beach-combing done here by the natives. The sprat-fishermen with their nets, people looking for driftwood or anything else of value they might find. Well, early this morning a man by the name of Lee was coming along past the Yacht Club when he saw something up ahead, not far from the Aquatic Club pier. Now in nine cases out of ten a native finding anything of value immediately appropriates it. For some reason that is not quite clear to me, this man Lee turned his findings over to an Aquatic Club attendant. He in turn gave them to one of my men who was in the vicinity making inquiries."

Scott watched the Major lean down behind his desk and bring forth two articles which, when separated, proved to be a towel and a feminine-looking robe. Right then Scott remembered the man he had seen on the

beach when he had rowed to the Aquatic Club to telephone Briggs, a Negro who had stopped to pick up
something that looked like clothing. He understood that
the man had probably done the honest thing because,
having been observed by Scott, he was afraid to do
otherwise. Even so he was not prepared for what followed.

"This is an Aquatic Club towel," Briggs said. "And
this robe"—he shook it out—"belongs to you, I believe,
Miss Reeves."

Sally's green eyes were focused on the Major now, her
face lovely in profile, the cheekbones no longer white.
When she spoke her voice was controlled.

"Yes."

"Did you leave it on the beach?"

"Yes."

"When?"

"I don't know."

Briggs frowned and there was a glint of exasperation
in his gaze. Before he could phrase the next question,
Sally elaborated.

"It was last night after I'd gone to bed but I don't
know just when because I don't know what time it
was."

"You didn't mention this in your statement," Briggs
said, still frowning.

"You asked me about the party. I thought that was
what you wanted to know, that and when everyone
left."

Her glance strayed to meet Scott's bewildered look
and she seemed to be censuring him, as though it was
his fault that she had not told the truth in the first place.
Then, as he sat there with the dismay and incredulity

growing in him, he heard the story of Sally's swim and
the oarsman in the dinghy who had tried to strike her
down. The recital of those details scared him, even
though the telling was done matter-of-factly and without emphasis; then there was only confusion in his mind
when he realized that all this had happened before he
went to her place to tell her about Julia and warn her
to be silent about the pillow.

Briggs had trouble too. He went over the story point
by point, giving particular attention to the time element.

"You went to bed but you didn't go to sleep," he said.
"You don't know how long after that you went for your
swim?"

"No. I'm sorry but I don't."

"You don't know who the man was?"

"No."

"Or if it was a man."

"I assumed it was but—I'm not sure."

"All you're sure of then is that someone was rowing
the dinghy towards the shore. When you hailed him he
attacked you."

The exasperation was still working on Briggs when
Sally nodded. He glanced at the others. Finally he stood
up.

"All right," he said crisply. "That will do for now." He
hesitated while chairs scraped and his audience came to
its collective feet; then he turned to Sally. "All except
you, Miss Reeves. I'm going to ask you to remain long
enough to give us another, and more complete, statement."

8

GODDARD'S was a second-floor restaurant-bar on a Broad Street corner and served as a meeting place for local shoppers as well as the passengers from the cruise ships which dropped anchor in Carlyle Bay. The most popular spot was the long veranda overlooking the street but Alan Scott avoided this and chose a corner table in the front room which was nearly empty. Having already made up his mind to do no drinking before evening, he ordered a "coke" and was still nursing it when the Farrows arrived.

Mark ordered a whisky and soda and Vivian a gin-and-tonic. She settled back, fanning herself with her straw handbag while her painted nails beat a soft tattoo on the chair arm. Her dark gaze had distance in it as it focused on some point outside the window.

"About the trip." Mark began to fill his pipe. "We may still be able to take it. I suppose it's idle to speculate on what the autopsy will show or—"

"It will probably show that someone murdered her," Vivian said. "Why else would anyone chase Sally with an oar in the middle of the night?"

"What I mean is," Mark said, ignoring her, "either the authorities will clear it up right away or they won't. If they do, well and good; if not I still think they might let us shove off after a day or two. After all we're reputable people."

"Darling." Vivian touched his arm. "Even so-called

reputable people sometimes stoop to murder, if one is to believe what he reads."

Farrow frowned and again clung to his thought as though there had been no interruption. He leaned muscular forearms on the table and said:

"No one would be likely to run for it. A few days needn't matter. If you've anything aboard that will spoil we could take it off your hands."

Scott spoke of the cooked ham and turkey. He spoke of other things while his mind moved on to speculate again about the murder and how little he knew of those involved. The Farrows, for instance.

Both had been married before. Mark was English and supposedly came from a good family, his manners and general attitude suggesting that his background and education had been more than adequate. Rumor had it that Vivian had married a wealthy Venezuelan while still a show girl in New York, and seeing her erect, high-breasted torso now, Scott could understand how desirable she could be to many men. He had seen her in a bathing suit the afternoon of the sail. She had a truly magnificent figure, she was an excellent swimmer—

His thoughts hung there as he remembered again the wet spots on the deck when he went below to find Julia dead in bed. He had thought then that some native bent on larceny had made them, but suppose someone with murder on his mind had chosen that way to come silently aboard, knowing that Julia lay defenseless in the forward cabin, not knowing Lambert was there but, finding him sound asleep, carrying out the plan regardless.

Such an act would, he knew, take nerve, but from what he had seen of Vivian—or Mark for that matter—

he knew they had it. He also understood that they had put all the money they had into the development of their Bahama island. They needed more and Lambert was to supply it.

Scott eyed the woman aslant as he made some comment to her husband, studying the strong-boned features, the smooth line of jaw, the set of the black, penciled brows. There was courage here; of that he was sure. Determination too, and loyalty for those who deserved it. Julia was not going to spoil the cruise. That was what Vivian had said. What she had meant was that Julia must not bully Lambert or prevent him from investing his money as he saw fit. And at the time everyone believed the woman when she said she was still married to Lambert.

Mark's voice interrupted the thought. Speaking beyond Scott, he said: "Hello Howard. Join us. What will you have?"

"Yes, Howard," Vivian said. "Do sit down and help us solve the case."

Crane pulled out a chair and sank heavily into it. He told the waiter he'd have a whisky and water and then he leaned back and looked from one to the other as he mopped his tanned face.

"It wasn't you, was it, Howard?" Vivian asked, still watching him. "I mean, if it was your secret is safe enough with us. We'd just like to know."

Her husband took the pipe from his mouth and looked aghast. "That's not very funny," he said reprovingly.

"Funny?" Vivian smiled at him. "I suppose not," she said, her tone conversational and carrying no emphasis. "I was just thinking that Howard chased around a lot with Julia last summer after she'd split up with Keith and while his wife was in England. I was wondering if Julia knew where the body was buried."

Mark opened his mouth and then closed it, as though such vernacular phraseology was beyond him. Crane took no offense. His blunt-jawed face was somber but his glance was remote as he shook his head.

"We had good times, too," he said in his "Bajan" accents. "She was quite good fun when she was sober. Drunk she was rather impossible." He hesitated, then grinned. "But I'm not the only one."

"Only one?" Vivian said.

"Who took her around. This Waldron fellow was pretty attentive too. He made it a competitive proposition, taking Julia to parties and things."

"Waldron?" Farrow glanced at his wife.

"You know the one," she said. "American. Talks as if he came from Brooklyn. Slender, dark, wears glasses, has a flat up St. Lawrence way."

"Oh, yes," Farrow said, and by that time Scott remembered how Frank Morgan had introduced him to Waldron the night before.

"It's not very pleasant though, is it"—Crane looked at Vivian—"knowing that unless it was accidental someone who was aboard last night killed her."

He signaled the waiter but Farrow had started to push back his chair. He said they had to be getting along. He waited for his wife to pick up her bag and just then Sally, Lambert and Freddie Gardner crossed a corner of the room and disappeared on the veranda. Apparently Scott was the only one who noticed because no comment was made. Instead Farrow said:

"I'll send a man for the turkey and ham. Somehow I still think we'll get that cruise in."

Scott sat down and Crane stretched his legs. When his drink came he said: "Chin-chin," and sipped it idly, making no effort to continue the conversation, his gaze detached and brooding. This gave Scott a chance to think about the man and his activities which, aside from an interest in a residential club and some local investments, were mostly social and sporting.

Few could call the man handsome but he had a lean, flat-muscled body that he kept in good condition. A man like Crane, Scott decided, would have no trouble scaling the vine-covered wall of the Carib Hotel; nor would Mark Farrow for that matter. Freddie Gardner, Scott asked himself as his thoughts moved on. Why not? The trouble was he had no proof that the prowler and the killer were the same person. . . .

"I'm sorry," he said, aware that Crane had spoken.

"I said a bit of news came in after you'd left the Central Station. I stopped in the Traffic Bureau to see a fellow and when I came out Sally and Keith and Freddie were just leaving. While she was making her statement word came in to Briggs that Julia really did get her divorce." He hesitated, his smile giving his face a lopsided look. "The police found the papers in her hotel room. The rest of it was sheer bluff on her part."

Scott took pains to register surprise. He made the proper exclamations.

"But what would be her point in lying?"

Crane shrugged. He said he did not know. "Except," he said, "Julia always had Keith pretty well under her thumb. He was afraid of her."

"He could have checked back."

"Eventually, yes. Being Keith it might be days before he got around to doubting her word. It would simply not occur to him. Meanwhile my guess is that Julia was after all she could get. With her around I doubt if Keith would be putting any money into Farrow's island—or anything else. At least not for a while." He beckoned the waiter and stood up to pay his check.

"In any case," he said, "it's the Major's problem now, and I imagine he'll settle it, one way or another. He's a very shrewd fellow."

Scott watched him go and then glanced round to find the room filling up. Women in cotton, sun-backed dresses came in for some rendezvous, most of them with straw shopping bags, many with children, some with both. The local business men were distinguishable by their white and tropical-weight suits and ties; the others were clad in slacks or shorts and for the most part wore loud-patterned, short-sleeved shirts. Those who were here on a holiday were at ease as they pretended they were residents of some standing; the others with their cameras, those here for the day from some ship, had more fun because they did not care what anyone thought.

Ordinarily the scene would have interested Scott but today he was brooding and saw little of it. He did see Lambert and Sally walk past the long bar on the way out and he did nothing to attract their attention. When they had gone he stood up and went out on the veranda where Freddie Gardner sat alone watching the activity on the street below. He glanced round when Scott pulled out a chair. He said he was having a rum and water and what would Scott have.

"Nothing, thanks," Scott said. "Just thought I'd sit down a minute."

Freddie made some comment Scott did not hear be-

cause he was busy with his own thoughts. He had asked
Lambert about Freddie once and he remembered what
Lambert had said.

"Freddie? I guess there's not much to know about
him. Been here a long time. Came from Trinidad or some
place but went to school in England for a bit. No money,
no family; at least he never mentioned any. Worked as
a greeter at various clubs, sold things, does some writing
for the *Advocate*. No great strength of character, really.
But then neither have I . . . Very amusing, Freddie. I
like him."

As these things came back to Scott he looked down
at the narrow, crown-surfaced pavement with its deep
gutters and wondered why anyone had named it Broad
Street. At its upper end it widened somewhat and was
graced by a half dozen modern-looking buildings but
the other way, towards the *Careenage*, the buildings
were old, two-storied mostly, their second floors overhanging the narrow sidewalks in many cases. Cars,
trucks, busses and bicycles rolled by in an unending
procession and diagonally across the way and next to
the department store was the alley which served as a
market place for the female hawkers to sell their vegetables and fruits, most of which were shipped in by
schooner from St. Lucia and Dominica. Somehow the
scene to Scott was ever changing, but as always the
smartest-looking individual performance was put on by
the white-jacketed and white-helmeted constable who
directed traffic with a flourishing precision that was a
delight to behold.

Scott saw all this even as his mind busied itself with
other things, and now he looked at Freddie. When he
had the other's attention he spoke without preliminaries,

his accusation low-voiced and intent but not angry. He said:

"You're the bastard who tipped off Briggs about the pillow, aren't you?"

Freddie's jaw sagged. He blinked hard behind his glasses and his round face flushed.

"What?" he said, his voice choked. "What did you say?"

"You were waiting there last night by the galley when Sally came out of the forward cabin. You heard what she said to me. You're the only one who could have heard."

"Well—I—"

Freddie broke off, swallowed. Then, getting himself in hand, he continued hotly, a defiant glint in his eye.

"Why not?"

It was Scott's turn to stare. He had not expected the answer and could not understand it. In his own mind there was no doubt about Julia's death being murder and he intended to ask why Sally had to be involved. Before he could say so, Freddie continued.

"Why shouldn't I tell the truth?" he demanded. "How did I know you were going to lie? You and Sally?"

"Wait a minute."

"Why didn't you tell the truth in your own statements? Why jump me just because I did?"

Scott eyed him scornfully and tried to keep his temper in hand. "You wanted Briggs to think it was an accident, is that it?"

"Why should I care what he thinks?"

"You're getting tough, huh, now that Julia's out of the way? Last night it was different."

"I don't see that—"

Scott cut him off. "If someone killed Julia deliberately —and I think someone did—it would be a wonderful break for the police to accept an accidental verdict." He leaned forward when Freddie tried to interrupt. "Julia despised you, didn't she?" he said, still quiet. "With her around your chiseling days were over. With her out of the way you've still got a living sucking around Lambert and trying to cut in on his deals. That makes a motive for murder in my book."

"Damn you." Freddie pushed back his chair. "You can't talk to me like that."

"I am talking to you."

"Not any longer, you're not."

With that Freddie was gone and Scott was sitting there wondering why he had to do things the hard way. Why couldn't he play it cagey and string Freddie along and try to find out what he thought about this and that. There were a lot of things he wanted to know. For one, he wanted to know more about this man Waldron who had known Julia so well the summer before. Freddie could have told him. But no, he had to start right out by accusing Freddie and Freddie would not stand still.

9

AT THREE o'clock that afternoon Alan Scott, flat on his back on the cockpit cushions, was staring at the sky and sullenly contemplating fate, circumstances, and his own unenviable plight. In the distance came the sound of bathers on the Yacht Club beach and now, hearing a splashing nearby, he assumed it was one of these until a familiar voice cut through his thoughts.

"Ahoy the *Griselda!* Anyone aboard?"

Sally Reeves was treading water twenty feet away and when she saw him sit up she waved and swam toward the ladder. In the next few moments while he helped her aboard and she stood sleek and dripping in her black one-piece suit he felt only the warm glow of pleasure that always came when she was near. Her hands were cold and soft in his but when she looked up her smile seemed forced and worry was working in the corners of her green eyes.

"I didn't see you but I saw your dinghy," she said. "I wanted someone to talk to."

He told her to sit down and she said she'd drip awhile first, standing where she was, firm-fleshed and slender, her young bosom rising and falling gently from her previous exertion. Normally it would have given him much pleasure merely to look at her and watch the simple movements of her body but when she sat down on the edge of the cushion and he began to think again this odd feeling of depression and futility began once more to warp his mood.

"It was Freddie who told Briggs about the pillow," he said. "He heard you tell me last night and I forgot that he was just round the corner."

"I wondered," she said, not looking at him. "I didn't know what to think this morning."

"I guess it was a bad idea, telling you to hold out on Briggs."

There was no answer to this. Sally was watching a small sloop come about beyond the Aquatic Club, or seemed to be. He was not sure she had heard him and after a moment he said:

"I'm sorry it didn't work out."

This time she heard him. She shrugged faintly, her gaze still fixed.

"It doesn't matter, Alan."

Again she was silent and now, his depression growing on him, he felt the first stirring of resentment.

"You might have told me about your swim last night."

"My swim?"

"The guy in the boat that chased you. That happened before I came to tell you about Julia."

"I know." She sighed, looked at him, dropped her glance. "I don't know why I didn't. I guess I was still scared. I guess I was thinking with my emotions instead of my head. When you told me about Julia and—the pillow—how she died—" She exhaled audibly. "You kept talking about that pillow and how we mustn't mention it. It was almost as if you thought I had killed her . . . oh, I know you didn't but—"

She cut the sentence short and Scott checked his reply. Why, he asked himself, couldn't she understand that until murder was proven the police must continue to suspect her. Or realizing this, was she afraid to admit it, even to herself?

When he saw she was still watching the sloop he tried to stop thinking and they sat mute and withdrawn until, with what seemed an obvious effort, she turned and gave him her attention. She managed a small smile. In her attempt to digress to more pleasant subjects she was even able to embellish her words with brightness, forced though it was, as she asked if he had heard the news about the divorce.

"Major Briggs said they found papers in Julia's hotel room which proved she actually had the divorce all the time," she said, interested now. "Imagine her telling Keith she didn't."

Scott said he'd heard about the divorce. What he said then surprised even him. He had no intention of sounding bitter, no desire to anger her. It may have been his own black mood, born of disappointment and frustration; it may have been self-pity, it may have been simple jealousy. Whatever the reason, he started off badly, and, having started, could not retrace his steps.

"I guess that sort of simplifies things, doesn't it?"

"Does it?" She eyed him curiously.

"Well, doesn't it? Now Keith can buy a piece of your sister's island if he wants to. If he wants to get married he can."

"What?"

Scott should have quit then. What he wanted most was to hear her laughter, to see her smile, to put his arm around her. Yet for all this some perverse and uncontrollable impulse kept him going.

"Well, isn't that how it is? You didn't come down here all the way from New York just to make a fourth at bridge on this cruise, did you?"

"Oh," said Sally and her smile grew tight and fixed. She looked right at him, her green eyes suddenly frosty. Understanding now what he meant, she seemed almost glad to have the chance to voice her resentment, and she promptly gave her attention to his question. "I'll tell you, Alan," she said, "since you're so interested."

He started to interrupt, seeing the danger signals and aware that he had gone too far. He flushed. He cleared his throat and tried to smile. But there was no interruption. She never gave him the chance.

"It's very simple, really," she said. "Vivian and I are step-sisters and we didn't have very good luck about keeping our parents. She lost her mother and I lost my father. That was a long time ago. Later my mother and her father were married and a few years after that her father died. We were never too close but Vivian was seven years older and she started to work as a cigarette girl when she was nineteen, and then she was a show girl in some of the better nightclubs because she had this straight and lovely body and a striking sort of beauty that is always in demand."

She hesitated, not looking at him now, her thighs together and her hands cupped on her knees. "She sent money to my mother and me after her father died. Later, just after mother passed on, she married a rich Venezuelan. She sent me to boarding school and then through four years of college and there was no way I could pay her back even though it was always in my mind. Her husband was killed in a plane crash and his money was mostly his family's and they offered her a hundred thousand dollars as a settlement. I was still in college then and I seldom saw her but the monthly check always came on time."

She paused and said: "She was twenty-eight when she married Mark Farrow. They were in love then and are now but I think there was a little misunderstanding about money. She did not have quite as much as he thought she had and it was the same way with him—a good family in England but not enough money of his own to retire on. So they got the idea of developing this island. They put all they had in it and a little more they got from friends. The trouble was it was more expensive than they guessed. They own the island. They have a dock and a comfortable fishing camp and roads. They think once they have a guest house and some cottages and maybe a nine-hole golf course they'll get the people they want."

"Look," Scott said, feeling uncomfortable and ashamed and wanting desperately to say he was sorry.

"No, Alan." She shook her head and her smile was still fixed. "You wanted to know, didn't you? . . . So they found out Keith Lambert had plenty of money to invest and Vivian called me. She said she needed help and for me to get time off and come down here. She sent me the fare and I came because I wanted to help, not knowing what she wanted until I got here. They had planned this cruise because they wanted to get Keith away from all the others who were after his money. All I had to do was be a pleasant companion for him while I was here."

She looked right at him and said: "If you think I was supposed to act as—what do you call it, a shill?—you're mistaken. The selling, if any, was to be done by the Farrows. Being a practical minded person Vivian suggested that I could do worse than marry Keith but that was her thought, not mine. All I had to do was look as pretty as possible and be agreeable to a pleasant young man who is very much of a gentleman even though not particularly adult. That's what I intend to do if we ever take the cruise. Furthermore I hope Keith will back the Farrows—I wouldn't say this to him because it's not my affair—because I think they have a sound investment."

She stood up then, putting on her cap as she did so. When he rose with her and put out his hand, she avoided it. By that time he was ashamed of his conduct;

he was ashamed of all those thoughts he had harbored
that made him doubt her.

"I'm sorry, Sally."

"It's quite all right." She gave him a smile but it was
a strange sort of smile and one he had never seen before. "As a matter of fact I'm glad you asked. I knew
something was wrong. I've been wanting to tell you how
things were and now you know."

"It wasn't any of my business," Scott said. "I don't
know what got into me. Maybe it's because I'm jealous
but—"

She did not seem to hear him. She was poised on the
rail now, starting her dive, and he said: "Wait!" and
she, speaking over shoulder, said: "I think you're having
company."

She hit the water then. When she surfaced and
started to swim he glanced round and saw the rowboat
coming with the police constable in the stern. He waited
until it came alongside, long-faced, disconsolate and irritable.

"Major Briggs would like to see you, sir," the constable said. "I'm to wait and accompany you."

10

MAJOR BRIGGS wasted no time on the amenities once
Scott had settled himself in the chair at the end of the
desk. His manner remained businesslike but his glance
was enigmatic and direct, and his opening remarks
came as a distinct shock.

"I'm afraid I'll have to ask you for another statement, Mr. Scott," he said. "That's why I sent for you. It would help matters if you'd tell the truth this time."

Scott's mouth opened and his angular face flushed. In that first instant he seemed unable to think and the best he could do was to make a parrot-like reply.

"Truth?" he said.

"According to your statement"—Briggs consulted the paper as he spoke—"you came aboard the schooner with Lambert about one o'clock. You remained there until after you had discovered the body somewhere around six this morning. Is that correct?"

Unable to make the direct lie, Scott hedged. "I think that's what I put down."

"How then do you explain your presence at the Carib Hotel shortly after three this morning?"

Briggs' tone was conversational but his eyes remained probing and suspicious and Scott knew he had very little time to make up his mind. He could deny the accusation, tell the truth, or stall. He decided to stall first.

"Who says so?"

"As a matter of routine," Briggs said, referring to some papers on his desk, "we checked every employee at the Carib to see if anyone had made any inquiries about Julia—I believe the proper name is Parks. There were no such inquiries but a man was seen to leave the rear entrance of the service wing and enter a car parked nearby at approximately three fifteen. Fortunately the license of the car was noted. According to the records the car is owned by Dear's Garage and is hired by you."

Scott let his breath out, deciding now that it was pretty silly to carry on with his bluff. It had been a mistake in the beginning, considering how things were

working out. He did not know how he could justify his
lie but it no longer seemed to matter, provided he could
keep from involving Sally any more than she was already
involved. He saw no reason for telling of his early morning call on her and the warning he gave and so, omitting
only this, he told the truth, finding it a great relief to be
able to do so.

Briggs listened without interruption and then asked
the obvious question. "Why wait at all? Your duty was
to inform the police at once."

Scott couldn't think of any answer. He stared glumly
at the desk top, suffering in silence until Briggs pressed
him for another answer.

"What did you expect to find in the woman's room?"

Scott said he did not know. Last night he had been
scared and confused. He had no thought of searching
Julia's room until he found the key in her pocketbook.
It was an impulse—a very bad one he was free to admit
—rather than sound judgment that made him go there
looking for some clue that might help.

"For all I knew," he finished lamely, "I might be under some suspicion, might even be arrested. Then it
would be too late to look."

"You *are* under some suspicion, Mr. Scott. More so
now than before." Briggs sighed and glanced out the
window. "It's not a very good answer, is it?"

"No," said Scott, "it isn't."

Briggs hesitated, eyes still probing. "You were alone
with her on the boat after the others left."

"For a few minutes."

"Long enough. And you thought she was still married
to Lambert, which gives you a motive."

"How?"

"You may have thought that with the woman alive Lambert might not buy your schooner, which I understand is important to you . . . It is, isn't it?"

"Well, I want to sell it, yes."

Briggs nodded. "When, exactly, did you discover the body?"

Scott told him and Briggs said: "Assuming you did not kill her she must then have died between 11:20 when you left the schooner, and 2:05. For the hour previous you were in your quarters and Lambert was asleep in the main cabin. What waked you?"

Again Scott had to say he did not know. "It may have been some motion of the boat, or some sound I don't remember hearing. When I saw the wet marks on the deck I thought some native might be prowling about. That's why I went below to have a look."

"Lambert was asleep all this time?"

"Let's say he looked asleep each time I saw him."

"Very good." Briggs nodded. He rubbed his palms together. "Now about this man who attacked you in the hotel room. You have no idea who he was? . . . You're quite sure?"

"Positive."

"What was the condition of the room, the bags particularly?"

Scott told what he remembered.

"You took nothing. You saw nothing to give you any idea why anyone should be searching her belongings?"

"There was some jewelry in the bag that wasn't opened. The divorce papers were there too but I don't know how anyone would know that beforehand."

"All right." Briggs took a cablegram from the desk and passed it to Scott. "Did you see this in the pocketbook when you took the keys?"

Scott scanned the message, which had been dispatched four days ago to Julia Parks at a New York address. In substance it said that if Julia intended to get down to Bridgetown before Lambert spent all his money she had better hurry. It was signed, Howard.

Scott shook his head. He said he had not searched the pocketbook. "Crane?" he asked, his stare perplexed.

"We think so. I intend to ask him . . . Ahh," he said as an aide entered and saluted, "here he is now."

Howard Crane came in, glanced at Scott and Briggs; then took the chair the Major indicated. Briggs took the message from Scott and handed it to Crane.

"I believe you sent that, Howard," he said.

Crane merely glanced at the sheet. He placed it carefully on the desk and leaned back. He nodded, his lopsided smile wry.

"Yes," he said. "I've been wondering about it."

"As a policeman," Briggs said, "it strikes me as odd, not so much that you should send the wire—though I don't know yet why—but that Julia Parks should arrive last night and be killed before morning."

"It strikes me as odd too," Crane replied. "That's why I didn't mention the cable before. I suppose you want to know why I sent it and I'll try to explain what I had in mind."

He offered a tin of cigarettes, lit his own and leaned back in his chair. "Keith's inheritance is the real reason. He never had any money, and all at once he has a potful which he seemed intent on spending. Everyone was eager to help him. The Bailey brothers have been after him to underwrite their real estate development. The Simmonses wanted him to back a restaurant, the Farrows wanted to sell him part of an island, none of which bothered me because my wife and I have enough of our own. What did bother me was Freddie Gardner's plan to enlarge the Flamingo."

He glanced at Scott, as though to clarify the reference. "I'm the principal owner of the Surf Club," he said, "and lately we've been doing quite well with our rooms. The Flamingo is almost next door to us. Freddie has a small interest in it, and big ideas. It's an old house which has been remodeled. There are six rooms to rent, and they serve meals . . . Right now," he said to Briggs, "they are on the thin edge. Freddie's idea is to get a hundred thousand from Keith, put up some detached rooms, modernize it to accommodate fifteen or sixteen couples."

He shrugged. "I don't want that to happen. There isn't enough business up there for two of us. The competition will damn well ruin us both. But Freddie's a pal of Keith's and he just *might* get that backing, and that's why I cabled Julia. Even divorced—and I thought she was—Keith would be afraid of her. He always was. Furthermore she always hated Freddie. I thought if I got her down here she'd see to it one way or another that Freddie didn't get that money. It seemed worth the try." He gestured emptily. "Telling it like this after what happened may not make much sense to you, Major, but that's why I cabled her."

Briggs nodded thoughtfully, his manner suggesting that he accepted the explanation. So did Scott. Crane's story was straightforward and his reasoning that Julia might have prevented the investment had been corroborated by others. The snatch of conversation he had heard on deck while the party was going on bore this out.

"As for that," Crane said, indicating the cable, "you can hardly blame me for not rushing in and telling you it was my fault Julia came. After all, I suppose I'm among the suspects and I haven't any alibi. I went home after I left Club Morgan but we have no servants sleeping in with my wife away, and I can't prove it."

"You're not alone in that," Briggs said dryly, and referred to his notes. "Lambert took Miss Reeves home. He talked with her a few minutes before he left and he would not have had time to go aboard the schooner and still arrive at Morgan's when he did. The crucial period for him is the hour when you"—he glanced at Scott—"were in your quarters. We've only his word that he was asleep all that time.

"Freddie Gardner," he continued, "says he went home after he left Lambert but there's no substantiation for that either. The Farrows went home. We know that because there was a party across the street and they were seen to come in at 11:35, which would be about right. But later, at approximately 1:30, their car was seen to drive off again; what we don't know is who did the driving."

"What do they say?" Crane asked.

"He says he went to bed—they have separate rooms —and she says so too. She says if anyone says he saw a car at that time he's mistaken—so there we are." He glanced at some papers on the desk, continued to Crane:

"By the way. What, in your opinion, was Julia Parks' reason for pretending she was still Mrs. Lambert? I understand you knew her pretty well. Did she say anything to you?"

Crane shook his head.

"The only thing I can suggest is that she was pretty bitter because she had divorced Keith too soon and decided to take a gamble in the hope of bluffing him. She had the faculty of making him do about what she wanted him to do. He could eventually check back and find out she was lying but I think she hoped to force some sort of financial settlement out of him before that happened."

As he finished the aide again came in. Scott did not understand what he said but Briggs seemed to. He nodded and said: "Ask him to come in."

He glanced at Scott and Crane. "We managed to find one other person who may shed some light on this business . . . Come in, Mr. Waldron. Have a chair. Do you know these gentlemen?"

Tom Waldron said yes. He said hello. He looked just as natty now as he had the night before when Scott had met him at the Club Morgan bar. He wore white buckskin shoes, yellow socks, and a well draped white tropical worsted suit, contrasting sharply with his dark skin and hair and dark-rimmed glasses.

"You know what happened to Julia Parks," Briggs said.

"Your man told me," Waldron said. "And it's a rough deal for Julia. I don't know anyone who liked living better than she did."

"You were quite friendly with her, weren't you?"

"For a while I was." He glanced at Crane. "Howard and I used to take turns taking her out last summer."

"Umm," said Briggs. "That's why I asked you to stop

in. I thought perhaps you might be able to tell us why
she was here and what her plans were."

Waldron crossed his knees. He shook his head. "I
didn't see her," he said.

"But you knew she was here."

"Well, yes. I met Mr. Scott at Morgan's and he told
me she'd just flown in. That was later—"

"I mean before that."

Waldron waited, his deep-set eyes revealing nothing
as he watched Briggs go through some papers on his
desk and finally locate the one he wanted. What Briggs
said then corroborated Scott's earlier opinion that it was
not only silly but a waste of time to hold out on Briggs.
He was not spectacular but long years of experience en-
abled him to utilize the resources at his command in a
manner that was both thorough and efficient. Now,
glancing at Crane, he said:

"You took Miss Parks to the hotel. You had some
drinks and dinner. To your knowledge did she make a
telephone call during that time?"

"Yes," Crane said. "Before dinner. We were in the
cocktail lounge and she said she had to make a call."

"She made it through the hotel operator," Briggs
said, giving his attention to Waldron. "There is a record
of such calls in case there is any question as to which
guest made what call later on. The number Miss Parks
asked for was yours, Mr. Waldron. According to my information she talked to you three or four minutes."

Waldron's mustache curved upward at the ends as his
smile worked at it. The gleam in his eyes may have been
one of respect.

"Bull's eye, Major," he said in his city accents.

"And what was the substance of your conversation?"

"It didn't have much substance. I was surprised she was on the island. I asked her how come and she said business. I said monkey business and she said no, financial business. I said: 'Okay, and what're you doin' tonight? How about meeting me for dinner?' She said she had a date and I said: 'All right, how about later at Club Morgan?' She said: 'I might just do that.'"

He glanced at Scott. "I was still waiting for her when I met you and what you said told me she wouldn't be making it."

Scott did not hear Briggs' comment. Common sense told him he was reaching a long way for suspects, but he was also aware that in Waldron there was one other who knew that Julia lay unconscious and defenseless in the forward cabin of the *Griselda*. As to the possible motive he did not speculate; it was enough for now to know that Waldron had the opportunity. Waldron had left Club Morgan right after Keith Lambert arrived. Time enough. . . .

"I'd like a statement to that effect," Briggs was saying to Waldron. "And yours too, Mr. Scott. You can use a desk on the veranda if you like."

"Is it all right to ask a question?" Scott said, remaining where he was. "Have you made any progress?"

"Some."

"What about the post mortem?"

"It indicates the woman died of asphyxiation."

"But she was murdered."

"If you mean deliberately," Briggs said. "We can't be sure—yet."

Scott was aware that his voice was rising even though he tried to keep it down. His impatience at Briggs' evasiveness was corroding his nerves and because the opin-

ion was so important to him what he said was not very
polite.

"Nuts. She damn well didn't smother herself."

"On the contrary," Briggs said calmly. "She may very
well have done just that. Miss Reeves used a pillow
to—"

"She tossed a pillow at her," Scott said, close to shouting now.

"Admitted. But there *was* a pillow." Briggs waved for
silence. "According to the doctors there have been cases
where persons intoxicated to the point of paralysis have
caused their own deaths. Men have fallen down with
their heads twisted against a stair or piece of furniture
at such an angle as to cut off the breath. They have
died that way, powerless to move or help themselves.
Others have died in bed, suffocated by bedclothes or
pillows because they were unable to move. Such ac-
cidents are not common but there is a possibility that
some such thing might have happened last night. Even
without pressure the weight of that pillow, over a period
of time, might have been sufficient to cause asphyxiation."

Scott heard every word of this and the implication
quieted him more than anything else could have done.
He did not believe it, not any part of it, but his argument was more despairing than enthusiastic.

"There was lipstick on that pillow," he said. "It would
take pressure to make those marks."

"That's hardly conclusive."

"And what about the guy in the dinghy?" he added,
as this new thought occurred to him. "Why should he
try to club Sally? Or," he added sarcastically, "maybe
that's just one of the quaint local customs."

Briggs recognized sarcasm when he heard it. Spots of pink grew in his cheeks but his gaze was steady, his manner tolerant as he replied:

"Suppose someone who had a motive for wanting to kill Miss Parks went out there last night to see her, not necessarily bent on murder but perhaps wanting to force a decision on some mutual problem. Such a person, finding her dead, might be afraid he would be accused of killing her. Certainly he would not want to be seen leaving the schooner. I can see how, in a moment of shock or panic, he might feel compelled to strike out at anyone who might be able to testify against him."

He spread his hands, palms vertical, as though to say he did not wish to be dogmatic about the matter. "Unlikely perhaps but possible, since one never can be sure how a certain individual will react under pressure and emotional stress . . . However"—he pushed back his chair—"it is not my place to argue the matter with you at this time. We are making progress, Mr. Scott, but we must consider all possibilities."

He stood up. "About your statements," he said, nodding also to Waldron, "you'll find paper and pens outside . . . Take your time, Mr. Scott," he added with what might have been a smile. "We'd like the truth this time, if you don't mind."

11

ALAN SCOTT saw the skiff tied to a stern cleat as he rowed out to the schooner but he did not know who his caller was until Keith Lambert untangled his skinny frame from the cockpit cushions and sat up to wave a half-filled glass in greeting.

"Hello," he said. "Hope you don't mind my helping myself."

Scott said that was what the whisky was for and wondered what came next. He got a "coke" for himself and sat down, resenting just a little bit Lambert's liberty in making himself so much at home, and in no mood for conversation. Neither, it seemed, was Lambert. Not for three full minutes did he speak. When he did he gave no hint as to the purpose of his visit.

"Been in town?" he asked finally in his odd tenor voice.

"Had a session with Major Briggs—at his request."

"Oh? Any startling developments?"

"I found out why Julia happened to be here."

Lambert had been looking idly across the water. Now his head came round and his brown eyes opened, wide and serious.

"You did?"

"Crane sent for her."

"Howard? But why—I mean what on earth—"

Scott put an end to the stammering by repeating the story Crane had told Briggs, and by the time he had finished he had Lambert's undivided attention. He had put his glass aside when he sat up, nodding from time to time, frowning. Now he pushed his blond hair back from his bony forehead.

"I can believe it," he said. "Freddie is what you chaps call a—a—"

He groped for the word and Scott supplied it.

"Chiseler?"

"Yes, that's it. I've known that right along but I happen to be very fond of him. It so happens I knew he wanted money for the Flamingo. Furthermore I can understand why Howard didn't want him to have it and Howard's the sort of chap who can do a bit of thinking even if he doesn't do much work. Howard has to look out for Howard, so to speak, and he was right when he said Julia would raise a fuss. She would have—with me, that is—no doubt about it . . . Still and all," he said, "it's my money, you know, and I think if I had wanted to throw in with Freddie I would have, Julia or no Julia. As a matter of fact, Howard needn't have worried. I don't think I would have put money into the Flamingo anyway, not with Freddie managing it. Freddie doesn't —well, I mean he simply doesn't have the knack of making a success of anything."

He stopped for breath, nothing in the cadence of his voice suggesting that he felt any animosity or resentment towards Freddie or Crane.

"Freddie didn't know that," Scott said. "That you weren't going to back him."

"He doesn't know it now. As for the Farrows, well until this tragic business with Julia happened, I'd thought theirs might be a most interesting speculation. I'd like something like that, something you could develop and be a part of. I thought if we could arrange a satisfactory arrangement I might well go in with them . . . Oh, yes. One reason I came aboard was to tell you —in case you've been worrying about it—that I think I'd still like to buy the *Griselda* if you care to sell."

Scott said he was glad to hear it. Normally he would have felt both relieved and excited by the news but he had been doing some thinking while Lambert was talk-

ing and there was no room in his mind for elation of
any sort. Somehow the *Griselda* no longer seemed quite
so important and the focus of his thoughts was centered about Sally and her swim, the man in the dinghy,
and suddenly, Luther, his mate.

Luther lived about a third of a mile down the beach
in a narrow, dead-end road that had access to Bay
Street. Luther spent much of his time on and about
that beach when he wasn't working, and Scott found
himself wondering if Luther might possibly have been
aboard last night.

Suppose someone other than Sally had seen the man
in the dinghy? Not the attack necessarily but just the
movement of the dinghy as it went out to the schooner
and back. Somehow it seemed important that he ask
Luther about this. Luther could make inquiries of
others who lived nearby and spent time on the beach.
Such an investigation, especially if made by a native,
might result in a lead of some sort that could be passed
along to the police. Somehow murder must be proved
and certainly the guilty one could not have all the luck.

A strange excitement began to work on him as he built
the premise in his mind and now, as his thought moved
tangent-wise, he remembered Waldron.

"Do you know a guy named Waldron?" he asked abruptly.

Lambert blinked at the digression. "Why, yes," he
said. "Not well, actually, but I know him."

Scott hesitated, wondering what to say. What he actually wanted was a dossier on Waldron but he could
hardly expect to get it. The most he could hope to learn
was what Waldron did in Barbados, what reason he had

for being here—not necessarily the truth but an accepted reason nonetheless—how he conducted himself.

"What does he do?"

"If you mean in a business way, nothing. Plays a lot of golf. He's up to the club nearly every afternoon. Swims. Gets around to various social dos." Lambert grinned. "After all what do most of you Americans do down here?"

"Most of them are older, the retired ones."

"Some come for their health if they can afford it. I understand that's why Waldron came. Asthma or catarrh or something. Maybe arthritis. Thought he'd try the climate. Liked it and stayed on."

"Any special women friends?"

"None that I know of. Sort of plays the field." Lambert frowned, as though reaching back into his memory. "I did hear he made his money in some sort of war surplus deal. Wouldn't be surprised. Seems like a shrewd one. No fool in any case."

Scott gave up. He wanted to think of more questions and there were none he could find. It annoyed him that this should be so because the information told him nothing and was singularly unsatisfying. Then, as the silence lengthened, his thoughts diverted to a subject that seemed always to be lurking in the back of his mind to torment him.

Sally again. And Lambert.

"Are you going to marry Sally?" he said, a little surprised at his own bad manners.

Lambert blinked. He laughed abruptly, a high-pitched sound.

"I'd like nothing better," he said. "She's a lovely girl. She likes me too; she said so. But"—he laughed again without bitterness—"as a husband I'm afraid I couldn't interest her less. I asked her. She said no."

Then, as though the statement settled all problems, he rose and climbed awkwardly into the skiff. As he pushed off he said: "Thanks for the drink." He started to take a stroke, stopped to glance back at Scott. Indicating another small boat angling towards them from the Aquatic Club he said: "Looks like more visitors. Mark Farrow, isn't it?"

Farrow was sitting in the stern of a club boat, a Negro at the oars. He called something to Lambert as the two passed and when, a minute later, the boat came alongside he jumped lightly to the deck.

"Thought it might be a good time to pick up that ham and turkey," he said, and turned to swing aboard two large baskets his Negro oarsman handed him.

Scott said he would take care of it, and how about a drink first. Farrow said thanks, that he could do with a spot of whisky and a little water.

"Don't bother with ice," he said.

When Scott came topside with the drink Farrow was packing his pipe. He said: "Cheers," automatically as he tasted the drink and then put it aside until he had his pipe going. He crossed muscular legs and hunched over his knees as he sucked smoke in small mouthfuls, a dark-browed, dark-eyed man, his close-cropped hair peppered with gray.

"I've been thinking about the cruise," he said.

"So have I," Scott said.

"Makes it difficult, not knowing how to plan. I suppose there's always the possibility that the authorities might insist that we stand by until they've made up their minds about Julia."

"I had a session with Briggs this afternoon," Scott said sourly. "He hadn't even decided whether it was murder yet."

Farrow said he was not surprised. He said the police moved more slowly here than they did in the States.

"The system is different," he said. "The results are usually the same but they go at things with one eye on the rule book and the book says proper form is perhaps more important than needless haste." He tasted his drink, relit his pipe which had gone out. "How much more time do you have?"

"Unless I get an extension to my leave, between two and three weeks."

"That should give us time," Farrow said. "I'd rather take a somewhat curtailed cruise than none at all; that is, if it's agreeable to you. But should the police prevent even that I want you to know that I will reimburse you for any and all expenses you've incurred."

"The five hundred advance more than covers that part," Scott said.

"That's all right then. I suppose one should leave it that way and stop crossing bridges."

Scott took the baskets and went below to pack the ham and turkey. When he came back he put them down and waited until Farrow finished his drink before he said this thing which had been shaping in his mind. That Farrow would probably heartily resent the attempt was not enough in itself to keep him from making the accusation.

"Was it you or your wife that took your car out around one thirty last night?"

Farrow gave him a blank look.

"I'm sorry," he said. "What was that again?"

"There was a party across the street from your house last night."

"Yes, there was. Noisy too."

"Briggs says that someone there saw your car leave about one thirty."

Farrow's brows were raised but nothing showed in his face.

"I'm afraid that someone is wrong," he said.

"It wasn't you?"

"Definitely not."

"And can you be sure about your wife?"

"I couldn't actually take an oath on it, if that's what you mean."

"Do you share the same room?"

"As a matter of fact, no. I snore some, so she tells me," he added frankly. "There's a dressing room between us."

"What I mean is, she *might* have gone out without your knowing it. You *might* have done the same."

Only then did Farrow seem to understand what Scott was driving at. It was not so much that he was slow-witted; it was more a question of manners, a reluctance to admit that Scott would have the nerve to make such an obvious insinuation. Color crept slowly up his sun-burned neck and his mouth seemed to stiffen.

"Are you suggesting that one of us killed Julia?"

"Someone did," Scott said, coloring a bit himself now in his persistence. "Someone came out here and held that pillow over Julia's face, and eventually Briggs is going to agree with me."

He paused to wait for some reply but Farrow was just watching him, unmoving and silent.

"It was an easy thing to do," he added. "And her

death simplifies things for a lot of people. It solved some problems."

"It made some too."

"But only temporarily. When it's all over Lambert can do as he pleases with his money. With Julia around it might have been different."

Farrow admitted this. He said he saw what Scott meant.

"You still need Lambert's help, don't you? I mean financially."

"Indeed yes," Farrow said. "Very much so."

And with that he rose and motioned to his boatman. He handed down the two baskets and followed them into the stern seat. As the Negro dug the oars in Scott asked himself what he had accomplished by asking questions that might well alienate his best customer. He answered himself too. Nothing.

The street where Luther lived was narrow and bumpy, the crushed coral stone showing through the black top with discouraging frequency. The small houses which lined it decreased in quality the farther one progressed from Bay Street but Luther's, about halfway to the beach, was better than some.

It was square, unpainted, and tin-roofed, its single front step no more than six feet from the edge of the road and its four corners supported by thick wood blocks to give it a stilted appearance like its neighbors. A sagging wire-and-slat fence marked the narrow boundary lines and extended to the rear to make a sandy backyard, populated now by six or eight chickens pecking for stones and scraps of food while a mongrel dog lay asleep in the shade of a breadfruit tree.

Luther's wife answered Scott's knock, and it was apparent as she wiped wet hands on her voluminous skirt that she was angry. She was barefooted and her broad dark face was shiny. She wore a bandana over her hair and when she spoke a gold tooth glistened from one corner of her mouth.

Scott had always had trouble with the language when spoken by the island Negro. Basically English, it was so bastardized by accent as to be almost unrecognizable except to the trained ear and it embarrassed him to keep repeating a question that, in the speaker's mind, had been explicitly answered. Words ran into each other, their endings unpronounced. The broadness of the accent gave even the most simple sentences a foreign sound so that the most Scott could get out of Mrs. Luther—if that was her name—was that her husband was not at home. There were, however, certain words which he could identify. One was, humbug. Something, it appeared, had humbugged her, or her husband—humbug being used in the sense of "fouled up." Rum was another word he recognized; also, New Yorker.

Scott backed away before the woman's wrath got out of hand. He identified himself and said if Luther returned to tell him that he, Scott, was looking for him. It seemed then that he had made a discouraging beginning but as he made the turn into Bay Street towards town, he saw up ahead a sign which said New Yorker Bar. When he parked opposite it he found the bar occupied the ground floor of a narrow, two-storied house with an overhanging balcony.

In the first minute as Scott walked in off the sunlit street he could see nothing at all but the dim outlines of a bar on his right. He could tell the floor was stone

and voices told him others were present. Gradually then
he made out the aproned figure of the bartender and
the small back bar. A half dozen black faces took shape
in the thick gloom of the interior and he found himself
regarded with curiosity and some suspicion as he asked
if he could have a drink of rum.

He did not blame them much. They were dressed as
working men in khaki, some with hats and some with
caps. This was their bar, their private club in a sense; he
did not belong and though they showed no open resentment they fell silent as he spoke to the bartender.
Each had a tin mug in front of him and the bartender
slid a duplicate in front of Scott. He knew he should
accept it but something inside him rebelled and so, a
little disgusted with himself in his unwillingness to do
as they did, he asked for a glass. The bartender, who
had said not a word, found one, rinsed it and put it
dripping on the counter. He measured out a jigger of
rum, pushed an earthenware pitcher of water within
reach.

"Ten cents," he said; no sir, no please.

Scott found a coin and sniffed the rum. "Smells good."

"Yes, sir." Pronounced *Yahsuh*. "Smells good but it's
de taste dat counts."

With that someone chuckled. Scott took a swallow
and smiled. "Tastes good too," he said, and it was true.
"Ask them what they'll have," he said, indicating the
others.

Any misgivings he had were quickly dispelled with
the offer. Mugs were emptied with alacrity and the bartender got busy while Scott put a bill on the bar. When
all were served he asked if they knew a man named
Luther.

Again someone laughed.

The bartender said: "Luther?"

"He works for me," Scott said. "Aboard the *Griselda*. I wondered if he was in this afternoon."

"Yes." The bartender nodded. "He say he work for you. You're from the States . . . Yes, he stop in."

"How long ago?"

"Can't hardly say. Maybe an hour."

"Did he say where he was going?"

"Didn't say."

"Did you happen to notice which way he was headed?"

"Albert!" The bartender spoke to some man in the shadows. "You saw him. Tell de man (*mahn*) which way he go."

"That way," Albert said, pointing towards town.

Outside once more Scott cruised slowly for two blocks until he saw another bar which was outwardly much like the first except for the sign over the door. This read: Cosmopolitan. Inside everything was much the same: the customers, the bartender, the rum, the accents. Even the information was similar and as a result Scott stopped twice more on this side of the inner harbor to ask the same questions. Luther, it seemed, was making a tour of his own, with brief stops for sustenance, the trail eventually leading to a place called the Palmetto.

A constable on Trafalgar Street gave Scott the directions, and when he had parked in the municipal lot, he cut through the gates outside the old gray-stone public buildings and came finally to a square into which several streets ran at odd angles. The Palmetto, which stood near one corner, was less cavernous than the other bars he had visited because it had little depth and its long side ran along the street, admitting more light through its two doors and one square window.

Laughter came from inside. Two women hawkers, their enormous baskets now empty on their heads, loitered outside to join in the repartee from their vantage point on the curbing. Their laughter was wide-mouthed and raucous, their enjoyment of the moment immense. They shifted their weight and slapped thighs in delight before they trudged off, hips swinging and sandals flapping.

Perhaps because the Palmetto was more centrally located and catered to a more heterogeneous clientele, little attention was paid to Scott as he stepped inside and ordered a rum. As before he had to ask for a glass but the bartender was more affable and showed no reluctance in answering questions about Luther, once Scott mentioned the *Griselda*. He was indefinite about how long ago Luther had been in but it had not been long.

"Seems like Luther said something about you," he said. "Talked about goin' to B. G."

Scott understood that B. G. meant British Guiana and he did not bother to correct the man by saying that Luther was really going to Trinidad, when and if the schooner sailed.

"Said he was goin' tomorrow."

Scott nodded as the bartender moved off to serve another customer. When he had a chance he asked the man if he had any idea where he could find Luther and the man said no, not right now.

"Tonight maybe," he added.

"Tonight?"

The bartender rummaged around behind the bar and

came up with a folded copy of the *Advocate*. When he found what he wanted he folded the paper again and shoved it across the bar, pointing to a two-inch advertisement.

"Might find him there," he said. "When Luther's entertainin' the rum like today he like to dance, specially when he have money in his pocket."

"He had money?"

"Plenty money."

Scott examined the advertisement which said, in bold face: *Dance . . . Thursday Night*. The details, in smaller type, proclaimed that all friends of Esther Kane were invited to a dance at such and such an address . . . Luke Donnelley's orchestra . . . Two bars . . . Refreshments . . . Admission: Gents $1.00 Ladies 50¢ . . . Dancing from 8:30 on.

Scott grinned. He said it sounded like a good time and he would like to copy the address down. The bartender tore out the announcement and gave it to him, or started to. Scott took hold of the edge of the paper, but when the man still retained his hold Scott glanced up to find the other's narrowed gaze upon him.

"You wouldn't enjoy yourself," he said quietly as he loosened his grip. "It's not for folks like you."

12

IT WAS nearly six when Scott returned to the schooner and as he stepped into the cockpit he saw the note pinned to the edge of the hatch. Its penciled message read: *Come out to my place for a drink. We'll go some place for dinner. Be there until nine anyway.* It was signed: *Howard.*

Scott went below, undressed and pulled on his trunks. When he came on deck the sun was almost down in the west, its light reflecting from the water to outline the point of land which jutted out beyond the Aquatic Club and adding a soft brilliance to the casuarina trees which bordered it. This was the time of day to sit on deck with a drink and gloat at one's good fortune, to marvel at the softness of the air and wonder why the colors seemed more vivid just before they faded into the deepening dusk, to feel a little sorry for those who must battle the rawness of spring in the north.

Such thoughts had come to him before in moments of self indulgence but tonight they lingered only briefly before he went over the side. As always the clear warm water refreshed him and when he rolled over on his back to watch a puffy sunlit cloud break up to the southward he found himself wondering who would be at Crane's for a drink. Not that it mattered. He could do nothing about Luther for some time and after a day of abstention a drink would be welcome; so would a word with Sally if he were lucky.

The Crane house stood high on a bluff overlooking the golf course and the south coast. Built of stone by slave labor in early times, it was of massive construction, gray and vine-covered now, with cellar walls six feet thick and broad, high-ceilinged rooms. It was dark when Scott drove past the high steps leading to the veranda and parked in the paved court. Light poured from front

windows but when he climbed the steps he saw that it
was the veranda which was in use.

Crane stepped up to greet him but because of the
shadows it took a while to count the roll. Voices said
hello and he answered as Crane led him to a table which
was serving as a bar. Here, with the light behind him,
he could see Vivian in the wicker chair by the railing,
Farrow and Freddie Gardner sitting with their backs to
the wall, Sally and Lambert on the settee at one side.

"I'm my own butler this evening," Crane said.
"What'll it be?"

Scott said Scotch and water would be fine. He said
it was nice of Crane to leave the note of invitation.

"It seemed like a good idea to have a quiet drink,"
Crane said. "Tomorrow the whole messy business will
be all over the *Advocate* and everyone we ever knew
will be clamoring for details."

"You're overlooking the important point, aren't you?"
Vivian said.

"What's that?"

"Just that unless the police decide to call Julia's death
accidental and blame it on Sally—"

"They can't," Sally said, tension showing in her voice.
"Because I couldn't have done it. I'll never believe it
and—"

"I know, darling," Vivian said. "That's what I mean.
When we rule out the accident what we have left is
murder, which seems to mean that one of us is guilty,
which also means our friends will have a grand time
wondering which one of us did the job. Won't that be
just lovely, watching their faces, trying to find out what
they're thinking—"

"Oh, stop it!" Farrow's tone was blunt and irritable.

"Well, it's the truth, isn't it?"

"Do we *have* to discuss it now?" Lambert said in his odd tenor voice.

"There should be some subject less morbid," Freddie commented.

"I thought," said Sally, "that the purpose of this gathering was to relax and have a pleasant drink." She rose and moved away from the settee. "Wasn't it, Howard?"

"What?" Crane glanced round. "Oh, yes. Quite. Yes, consider the subject closed. Any further discussion will be ruled out of order."

"Hear, hear," said Freddie, and giggled.

All of this sounded forced and unconvincing to Scott. The tension was still there, touching all of them, building again in the silence that followed. If, as seemed likely, one of them was guilty, he knew the tension must be almost unbearable to that person, faced as he was with the task of watching every word and presenting always a show of innocence and unconcern.

Then they were talking again, Farrow moving over to sit next to Lambert, Crane looking about for drinks to refresh and urging his guests to drink up. Scott moved over and leaned against the railing beside Vivian's chair. When he asked if he could fix her drink she said no; she was fine, thank you.

"I understand Tom Waldron was down to see Major Briggs," she added presently.

Scott said yes, and explained why Waldron had been summoned.

"I knew he was rather friendly with Julia last summer," Vivian said.

"What else do you know about him?"

"Very little actually." She hesitated. "About the only

thing I know for sure is that he's a very good dancer."

"You never knew him in New York?"

"No."

"Somehow he doesn't look much like the retired-busi-
nessman type."

"No, he doesn't, does he?"

"But he has money."

"Some."

"Not a lot?"

"I don't think so. Mark talked to him about the island
once on the off chance that he might be interested. I
guess he was in a way but when it came to the matter of
investing he said his money was pretty well tied up . . .
I believe I will let you fix this," she said and offered her
glass.

Scott fixed a fresh drink and when he came back he
asked about the island. She asked if he knew Cat Cay
and he said no but he'd read about it.

"Well, we hope ours will be like that some day. It's
coral, of course, and close to some of the best fishing in
the world. We have a jetty up and some boat slips, a
sort of marina, with a comfortable camp, and we hope
to put up some cottages this summer . . ."

She went on with her description of the project and
Scott listened with part of his mind while the other part
strayed in patternless fashion. Freddie had gone over to
talk to Sally, and Lambert and Farrow seemed to be
arguing on the settee. Then, without warning, there
came one of those unexpected and often embarrassing
silences that occur from time to time in any social gathering. One instant the air was filled with the buzz of
conversation; the next there was only silence, and into

this gap there came a statement from Lambert that he was unable to check.

He did not speak loudly but the silence made it seem so. There was pique in the phrasing of his adolescent-sounding voice and his words were distinct and unmistakable, though the last one faltered as he tried to lower his tone.

"—never said I would invest."

That was what Scott heard and now the silence struck again. Lambert looked round, the darkness hiding his embarrassment. Everyone looked back at him. Scott could almost feel Vivian stiffen in her chair. Then, slowly, she sat up.

"Sorry," Farrow said stiffly. "Perhaps I misunderstood you."

"It's all right." Lambert was still truculent. "It's just that I don't like to be badgered."

"Badgered?" Vivian waited until she had Lambert's attention. "Surely not by Mark. He's not the badgering kind."

"I'm sorry," Lambert said. "It's just that, well—I haven't made up my mind."

Freddie tried to smooth things over. "I move and second that all business conversation be ruled out of order."

"So ordered," Crane said.

"We're all a little nervy," Freddie continued. "Good God who wouldn't be? Twenty-four hours ago everything was fine. We were going to Morgan's for dinner and have a nightcap aboard and then this morning we were going on our cruise. Then *she* came."

"Now *you're* out of order," Crane said. "Look. Let me

make a motion. What we need, when we finish our drinks, is some food. A good steak."

"Yes," Vivian said. "But please, not at Morgan's. By now he'll have the news—he always manages to know everything that happens—and I'm not sure I could face it tonight."

"We'll eat at the Surf Club," Crane said. "I'll phone for a table while you're finishing your drinks. "Let's see, seven of us, right?"

"Six," Scott said. "I have to see a fellow a little later."

He had a chance to talk to Sally when Crane went inside. "Still mad at me?" he asked.

"When was I mad at you?"

"This afternoon."

"I wasn't mad."

"Miffed?"

"Maybe a little."

Her eyes, as she looked up at him, were in shadow but the soft curve of her mouth told him she was no longer annoyed with him. He pressed her hand and let it go. He said he was sorry.

"I talk too much," he said. "Also I was jealous. I didn't mean to be but—"

"And you're not any longer?"

"Well, maybe a little."

"Good. Just so it's only a little. I like it that way. It's flattering . . . And you really can't eat with us?"

Scott said he was sorry and then Lambert came up to ask if she was ready. He was all right now, smiling, affable, attentive. Yet when Scott followed them down the steps he could not help wondering what had happened to this rich young man. Something had changed him; that much was certain. The brief scene with Farrow was proof that something was bothering him but Scott could not tell whether this had come as the natural result of the strain which had been working on all of them or whether the answer lay in something more important and deep-seated.

There was a brief argument when they gathered around the cars as to who was to ride with whom. In the end it was decided that Freddie would drive his car round back and leave it to be picked up later. It was when he turned on his lights and started the motor that Scott noticed the cracked lens with the missing piece. He waited somber-eyed and serious as the ancient car swung out of sight, aware that he had noticed a cracked lens like that before but not knowing just where. As he drove away the impression remained that he had seen that car somewhere the night before. Eventually the answer would come to him, though he did not expect it to matter much.

13

THE CLUB MORGAN was practically empty when Alan Scott arrived there at eight thirty. Only two cars stood in the parking lot and the attendant was not yet on duty. Inside the main room was quiet, so was the bar. A young couple sat close together at one end sipping martinis, and over behind a pillar and only partly visible a man was having dinner alone. Scott put all three of them down as newcomers to the island who had not yet learned that almost no one ever came to Morgan's for dinner before nine and that most people did not get around to eating before ten or ten thirty.

Abe, the headwaiter, was reading a novel in the little room to the right of the foyer and when he saw Scott he put the book down and followed him to the bar. Abe apparently had heard about the death of Julia Parks and when Scott had ordered a drink Abe was ready for details. A white-haired man of indeterminate age and antecedents, he had a soft and sometimes a profane way of speaking, his accents suggesting a one-time exposure to the cockney. Now his manner was respectful but curious, with just enough reluctance in his approach to take the edge from his persistence.

Scott said what he had to say, answering some questions and pleading ignorance to others. He said he imagined Abe knew Julia pretty well and Abe said yes indeed. Julia had been a frequenter of the club, first with her husband and later with Crane and Waldron.

"Quite a girl," he said. "Pretty in her way, and full of beans. Loved a good time, loved it."

"And her liquor."

"That too. Funny thing about that. At first you didn't think anything about it. I mean, she didn't drink any more than anyone else. It was only later after Lambert moved out that you noticed it. Gave us a bit of trouble now and then but gave her escort more when she put her mind to it. Yes, sir, a fine looking woman when she first came down here and opened her dress shop."

He shook his head and sighed. "Knowing her like that it's hard to imagine her smothering herself in bed. You'd think she was too rugged, too vital for that. Something violent you could understand but—"

He let the sentence dangle and Scott said: "She was

drunk. She was helpless. She never knew what happened. According to Major Briggs the medical books have described such cases before."

"What do the police think?"

"If by police you mean Briggs, he isn't saying. At least not to me. If you want my opinion, you can have it. I think she was murdered . . . Look, could I get one of those good hamburg sandwiches you have, with a few french fries?"

"For dinner," said Abe looking horrified.

"I haven't got time for dinner. I may stop in again later."

Abe asked how he wanted the hamburg and Scott said medium. Then he saw the bartender drain a fresh martini into a glass and place it in front of him.

"From Mr. Waldron, sir," the bartender said.

"Waldron?"

"Over there." The bartender pointed towards the column which hid the solitary diner.

Scott stood up and took a step to one side. That told him the diner was Tom Waldron. He gestured with his glass to acknowledge the favor and Waldron nodded and waved one hand. As a result Scott did a bit of thinking about the man while he ate his sandwich. Even after Waldron had left his thoughts centered on the ex-New Yorker, and it was not until he paid his check that he remembered there was information he needed before he could go looking for Luther. When Abe came back Scott showed him the advertisement of the dance that he hoped Luther might attend.

"Do you know anything about these things?" he asked.

"Not a great deal," Abe said. "It's a way for an en-

terprising woman with a lot of friends to make a few
bob."

"Would it be all right to go?"

"For you?" Abe chuckled. "What on earth for? You'll
be the only white man there."

"I thought it might be interesting."

Abe remained silent, an indication that he was not
so sure.

"There wouldn't be any trouble, would there?" Scott
asked.

"I don't expect so. Some of them might resent it a
little. I doubt if anyone would make a row, so long as
you didn't dance with some young buck's girl. You
might see a fight or two but you should be nimble
enough to keep clear of it."

Scott examined the advertisement again. He pointed
to the line which said there would be two bars, adding
that it must be a big dance.

"Not necessarily," Abe said. "It's the usual thing.
One's a liquor bar, the other's a pork chop bar."

"Pork chop bar?"

"That's the local term. Actually it means a food bar.
They cook up a mess of pork chops in advance and have
them there cold for the hungry. Bread and stuff. Maybe
fish or sandwiches." He grinned. "I'll wager fifteen minutes of that dance will be sufficient for you, but you can
see for yourself."

He supplied the necessary directions on how to reach
the address mentioned and then, motivated by some
impulse he could not explain, Scott thought of Waldron
again and asked if Abe knew where he lived. Abe did.

"Down near the end of Bailey's Gap on the St. Lawrence coast," he said. "Place called Mar-Vista or some

such name. Three brown-colored buildings, two bungalows and a two-storied house with four flats. Waldron
has the bungalow on your right as you face the sea."

Scott thanked him. It occurred to him then that in
Abe's position he might know other things about
Waldron as yet unspecified to others, but right now the
germ of an idea was beginning to blossom out of the
original impulse which had made him wonder about
Waldron in the first place. It was not, however, until he
was in his car and on his way that he knew what he
wanted to do.

He argued with himself all the way to the St. Lawrence coast. He admitted that he had nothing more to
go on than a simple hunch which kept insisting that
Waldron might know a great deal more about Julia and
the reason for her sudden visit to Barbados than anyone
suspected. But even if this were true there was no way
Waldron could be made to talk unless confronted by
some tangible evidence that had to be explained.
Waldron was, it seemed, something of a mystery man
and what Scott proposed to do now was something
that is known technically as breaking and entering, his
one forlorn hope pinned on the chance that he might
discover a motive for murder.

The idea appalled him even as he parked his car well
back from the Mar-Vista development and considered
the small, darkened bungalow to the right of the main
building. He had never considered such a thing in his
life and right now he did not even know what he was
looking for. The other night he had entered Julia's hotel
room with a key in his hand and the experiment had
ended none too happily. This was worse because he not
only had no key but could not, if asked, give any good

reason for his act. Even the police were forbidden to make a search without a warrant and yet—

He got out of the car and it may have been the thought that he lacked courage to make the attempt that stiffened his resolve and directed his feet towards the sand-colored coral building. There were lights on in the larger building but he saw no one about and heard no sound but the crunch of the waist-high surf breaking upon the beach.

The bungalow had a front veranda and a small back porch. It stood well off the ground, supported by concrete blocks, and its side windows had awning-like wooden sun shades which gave them a hooded look. He saw as he circled in the darkness that two windows were open. A wire boundary fence close by the right wall gave him the foothold he needed to reach the sill, and a few seconds later he had hauled himself upward and into the room.

It gave him a strange feeling, standing there furtively in someone else's house. It scared him a little, not the thought of what might happen but just the idea of being there unlawfully. He waited, not knowing which way to turn, the ceaseless sound of the surf in his ears, aware that he had no flashlight and could not very well do his searching with matches. The window hoods prevented anyone from seeing inside from an upper level and he realized now that the lower half of the windows were painted for opaqueness. By closing them he could look about without being seen. As for showing a light, that was a chance he had to take.

He saw the floor lamp as his eyes adjusted themselves to the darkness, and when he had closed the window he turned it on to find himself in a large high-ceilinged bedroom. There were two painted metal beds, each with a folded mosquito net hanging overhead. The furniture, of local design, consisted of a chest, a bureau and a vanity, two straight-backed chairs, a night table and a huge and ancient-looking wardrobe.

Of the two doors opening from the room, one led to the bath, the other into a small hall. Turning right he found himself in a living room that extended the width of the building and again he made sure the windows were down before he switched on a light. One end of the room was used for dining purposes, for there was a polished native-mahogany table, a sideboard, a half dozen matching chairs. The rest of the room was furnished with the sort of things which were indigenous to the climate and the island: cushioned wicker chairs, canvas chairs, a settee, some odd tables and a desk resembling a knee-hole desk but very little like it since instead of drawers on either side there were two doors.

Still not knowing what to look for or where to start, and continually prodded by his conscience, he stepped to the front door and opened it. When he saw the spring lock he pressed the catch so it would be on latch before he closed it.

His inspection of the desk did not take long once he had opened the side doors and saw the shelves inside. There was some stationery here, envelopes and paper, some folded newspapers, some clippings, a road map of the island. He examined none of this closely because he did not expect to find anything valuable or incriminating in a place so easily accessible, and having assured himself that there was no other likely hiding place here, he returned to the bedroom.

He went first to the wardrobe. There was a key in this

but it was not locked, and when he opened the doors he saw that it was literally full of suits, slacks, and jackets. On the floor were two pieces of airplane-type luggage. These indicated that Waldron had been traveling light when he came, that much of the clothing was the product of local tailors, acquired since his arrival. One of the bags was empty but the other was locked, and when he shook it things bumped around inside.

He put the bag back, wanting to force the lock but not quite daring to. Apparently that bag was Waldron's way of keeping certain valuables beyond the reach of any curious or light-fingered servants, but Scott was not interested in valuables as such so he closed the doors and stepped over to the chest. Under stacks of handkerchiefs in the top righthand drawer he found two checkbooks and immediately gave them his attention. Here at least would be a record of what Waldron was doing with his money and for the first time a small stir of excitement began to make itself felt.

Thumbing quickly through the first, flimsy book which had been issued by a local bank he saw that most of the checks had been drawn to cash, with now and then a voucher made out to local merchants. The second was a product of a New York bank and he just started to examine its vouchers when, unaccountably, he stopped, head up and breath suddenly held.

Why?

This is what he asked himself and there was no answer beyond the feeling that somehow something had changed. He had not been aware of any such change but the feeling remained that it had happened.

He stood stock still, head cocked as he listened to the

crunch and slap and swish of the breakers outside. There was no other sound, yet some intuitive strain was pulling at his nerve-ends as though to warn him something was wrong. When that intuitive pressure continued he closed the drawer and stepped back. It was then that he noticed a draft in the room where none had been before, a swirling of cool air that touched his ankles and spiraled up his calves.

Turning then, he faced the hall door. On tiptoe he moved silently towards it, breath still held. He stepped across the threshold, turned right, then stopped, every muscle tense.

Waldron stood waiting just inside the living room, his tanned face tight and one shoulder lowered slightly. His left hand was in his jacket pocket, the thumb showing. His right held a small automatic that was pointed right at Scott's belt line.

For two long seconds they stood that way, silent, rigid, staring; then Waldron's shoulder moved and he stepped back into the light of the living room.

"Well, what do you know," he said. "Come in, pal. Come in."

Scott let his breath out and felt his muscles go loose. He could almost feel his body sag as he walked slowly forward. Waldron backed to the desk and slid a thigh across one corner, the gun still in his hand.

"I figure I'm going to grab me a native thief," he said, "and it turns out to be you."

"So?"

"So they put people in jail for stunts like this, even guys like you."

"On what grounds?"

"Breaking and entering."

"The door was unlocked. I was looking for you. I walked in."

"That's right, it was. The door I mean. Now tell me the lights were on when you came."

"They were," lied Scott.

The reply made Waldron think. His deep-set eyes narrowed behind the dark-rimmed glasses as he considered the possibility that someone might have been here before Scott. For another second he hesitated, gaze bright and steady, his mustache stiff-looking on his upper lip. Abruptly he slid off the desk.

"Wait here!" he said.

He walked past Scott, the automatic swinging down. He went into the bedroom and for a moment or two there was the sound of drawers opening and closing. When he came back he resumed his perch on the desk and this time when he spoke his city-bred voice was harsh and demanding.

"What the hell do you want?"

"I've been wondering why Julia was in such a hurry to get in touch with you last night."

"Maybe she liked me. Let's say she wanted a date."

"Not last night. She had a date. Crane."

"You think I killed her?"

"Just wondering."

Scott sat down and pulled out a cigarette. While he lit it he studied Waldron. Someone had said he was shrewd, was no fool, and Scott found himself agreeing. He also sensed that this was a different Waldron from the one he had talked with before. Here, under some pressure and with no need to make an impression, he reminded Scott of men he had seen hanging around corners on Broadway or Seventh Avenue; the gamblers, the sharpshooters, the idlers with no visible means of support.

Waldron had picked up some polish since he had been away but underneath he was the same person. Scott also felt that deep down there was something hard and compassionless in the fundamental character of the man, that he would do what he had to do to protect himself and his interests regardless of the consequences. For all of this, Waldron no longer worried him.

"Why do you think she came here?" he asked.

"To put the bite on young Lambert for as much as she thought she could get in a hurry. Why else?"

"That's what I've been wondering about. I've got a theory." Scott paused, grinned crookedly and made up the theory as he went along. "Julia divorced Lambert too soon. She cut herself off from a lot of money, and it was her own fault. I think the more she thought of it the more bitter and frustrated she became. I agree that she came down here to throw a bluff and try to collect but I'm wondering if there wasn't more than one string to her bow. Considering her frame of mind, if there was anyone else she could collect from or blackmail, I think she'd take a crack at it."

"Me for instance?"

"Possibly. You or Crane or Gardner; maybe Farrow for all I know. After all, who knows anything about you except what little you've told. Maybe Julia knew a little more."

"Okay."

Waldron nodded and his lips thinned out. Heretofore he'd had himself in hand. Scott did not know whether the change came because there was some truth in what had been said, or whether it was a simple resentment that anyone might feel when someone pried into his personal affairs. Whatever the reason, anger began to show through, in the voice which until now had been flat and untroubled, in the glint of his eyes.

"You're looking for trouble, hunh?" he said. "Okay, I'll give you some. You're pretty nosey, Scott. I don't like nosey guys. Let's get the cops up here and you can tell them your story. Then I'll tell 'em mine."

He glanced at the telephone and Scott waited, saying nothing, hoping he seemed unimpressed as Waldron continued.

"Maybe I can't make a breaking and entering complaint stick but they have other laws in this place. I read the paper and I know they got a thing like unlawful presence on private property. Keeps the native prowlers in line. You could be tapped for that. You don't have to break and enter, just being on someone else's property is enough. You go before the magistrate and he fines you and if you don't like it you can wait for a higher court."

"All right." Scott ground out his cigarette. "When the police come you can tell them about that automatic."

Waldron glanced down at it as though he had forgotten he still held it.

"According to customs it's illegal to bring a gun in. That looks like an American gun to me. Let's both go before the magistrate, hunh?"

It was a good bluff. He made it sound convincing and he could almost see Waldron's mind grappling with the challenge. When nothing was said he stood up, straightened his jacket. Still bluffing he walked to the door, opened it, and stepped onto the porch without a backward glance. As he went down the steps he heard the telephone ring.

Scott sat in his car for a few seconds after he had started the motor. Now that he was alone he felt weary and discouraged and a little annoyed with himself because he had been trapped like a common thief. He had accomplished nothing and knew very little more about Waldron than he had in the beginning. A hunch had brought him here and the only encouraging aspect of the incident was that somehow that hunch remained; if anything Waldron's manner and reaction had served to strengthen it.

He was in no hurry as he backed round and turned into the hard-topped road. He took it easy all the way to Highway 7, braked for the stop sign, swung left. What he did not know was that, halfway to town, a car came up behind him, dropped slowly back and then proceeded to follow at a safe distance through the almost deserted downtown section and out along the road to Esther Kane's dance.

14

HAD IT not been for the music which rocked the lodge hall where Esther Kane was holding her dance, Scott might not have found it. The directions Abe had given him were sufficient to put him in the right neighborhood, but it was only when he stopped at an intersection to put his head out the window and read a road sign that he heard the orchestra and was reassured.

This part of Bridgetown was unfamiliar to him even in daylight. Now it was as though the character of the city had changed with the coming of night. Landmarks were obliterated. The neighborhood stores were shuttered and dark and the overhead lights on an occasional corner served only to make the unlit places more confusing and obscure. He had turned right off Roebuck and climbed a winding hill, wheeling right near the top to come to this section of small, squarish shacks that stood in tightly packed and darkened rows. Now, guided by the music, he saw the lighted porch ahead and pulled to the side of the road to park the little sedan.

The music came to him clearly when he cut the motor and he stood beside the car a moment, listening to the solid calypso beat and, for some reason he could not explain, having no enthusiasm for the assignment he was about to undertake. This was not the white man's part of town and this was not a white man's dance. Even though there was no color line on the island he understood that his presence would probably be resented and it was only the thought of Luther that made him go. Somehow it seemed important that he talk to Luther this very night and the only way to do this was to go where Luther was.

The sight of the two constables standing together under the corner arc-light beyond the hall was reassuring and he wondered again about the uniform they wore at night. In daylight, when anyone could see, they wore spic-and-span white jackets and white pith helmets; at night with visibility obscured, especially when one drove a car, they wore their blue-black trousers, thick and wooly-looking, with hip-length capes of the same material, and garrison-type caps, also blue. This dark

monochrome of clothing together with their dark faces
made them almost impossible to see until one was nearly
upon them and it always surprised him that the authorities did not recognize the danger when these foot constables patrolled the roads.

This time one of the two had a bicycle and as they
separated he rode off to the right while his colleague
started down the highway towards Scott but on the other
side of the street. Then Scott was in front of the one-
story, white-painted building, starting up the steps to
the porch and the open double-doors beyond.

The porch was moderately crowded. Men sat on the
railing or leaned against it while other men and women
stood about in small groups, their talk and laughter bat-
tling the orchestra on even terms until they noticed him.
Then, one by one, the groups grew quiet. Scott could feel
their stares as he stopped in front of this woman who sat
behind a table placed by the doors, a plump woman in a
candy-striped dress who watched over a box of tickets
on one side, a box of money on the other. The mouth
which had been twisted in laughter a second or two before turned sullen as Scott put his dollar down in front
of her and her dark gaze was suspicious.

"They's nothin' here for you, man," she said, giving
the word *man* its characteristic broad accent.

"I don't expect to dance," Scott said. "I'm looking for
a friend."

She considered the statement a moment, one eye on
the bill. Finally she swept it into the box and tossed a
yellow ticket on the table. A tall Negro standing just inside the doorway took it away from him, tore it in two,
returned half; then Scott was inside, looking bewilderedly about this long low room that was hot with the

smells of rum and fried food and cheap perfume and perspiration.

On his left stood the two bars, as advertised. Made from planks stretched across saw horses, which in turn stood on boxes to give them height, the food bar came first, and as Abe had said, he could see the platter of pork chops, no longer full, the slabs of bread, the ribs, the mound of breaded pieces of meat or fish which he could not identify. It was slow going to avoid the dancers and pick a careful path through or around the bystanders, but he came finally to the liquor bar with its cases of soft drinks stacked behind it and the dark bottles of rum on the table which served as a back bar.

Two bartenders worked here, laughing and talking to their customers until they noticed Scott. His presence quieted them and he could almost hear the word being passed from drinker to drinker as they turned to look over their shoulders at him, not insolently but with studied care. The bartenders did not look at him directly after that, but from the corners of their eyes, and he kept his place until finally one of them stepped up and asked if he wanted something.

"Rum and water."

The man served him with dispatch: a paper cup—surprisingly enough—the rum, the water.

"A shillin' for the rum," he said when Scott asked. "Thruppence for the cup."

The money in hand, he ignored Scott. His grin came back as he turned to his regular clientele and presently all the talk and laughter came back, as though, for all they were concerned, Scott did not exist.

With his back to the wall near an open window, he sipped his rum and looked for Luther. This proved to be a difficult task because the hall was crowded with dancers and there was so much to hold his attention. The orchestra was a six-piece outfit and made up in volume what it lacked in finesse. The cornet was shrill and brassy, the clarinet stuck mostly to the high register. These two carried the ball against a background of piano, guitar, bass and drums, the dancers loving every note of it.

There was no accepted pattern to the gyrations of the couples on the floor. A few danced as one might do at home to a fox trot, others were locked in tight embrace, some weaving and bobbing, some shuffling steadily with a minimum of movement. By far the greatest number, at least on this particular piece, jumped about with joyous abandon in what to Scott seemed like a combination of the jitterbug and polka that had the floor shaking.

And all the time the pattern of his search kept repeating itself. He would start to concentrate on finding Luther and then some particularly acrobatic display would catch his eye and he would watch. It amused him to be here but it was disconcerting too to find himself the object of an almost continuous scrutiny as more and more dancers became aware of his presence. He found himself constantly avoiding the fixed stares, of letting his glance rove, always conscious of the colorful dresses of the women which ran to striped and figured cottons with here and there a plain color, usually vivid. Many of the men wore hats, even when dancing, and it bothered him that he found the glistening faces so much alike.

When the dance ended he still had not seen Luther and he waited right where he was, sipping his drink, lighting a cigarette as others were doing, never staring at anyone if he could help it. The crowd grew around the

bar. The floor never emptied but some went through a
back door to some open space beyond.

Minutes passed and as his impatience grew he moved
slowly around the perimeter of the room, scanning faces
without appearing to. He glanced out back and saw the
yard there and the trees and the fence which opened at
one side on a narrow alley. He came back towards the
bar and there in the front was Luther. He wore a tan
drill suit and a necktie. He seemed to be weaving slightly
on his feet and one arm was loosely draped about the
waist of a slender, brown-skinned girl in a blue polka-dot
dress.

By that time the customers were lined up three-deep
so Scott stood off to one side and waited for his chance.
He was still waiting when the band kicked off on a one
step. He saw Luther and the girl push through the outer
rim of drinkers and step onto the floor, and because he
was afraid to elbow his way too forcibly through the
press surrounding them he was unable to reach Luther
in time.

But having located his man, he kept his eye on him.
When the first piece was over and the crowd stood clap-
ping, he reached Luther's side and touched his arm.

"Luther," he said. "I'd like to see you a minute."

Luther, it seemed, was quite drunk. He did not even
glance round. "Don't bother me, man," he said. "I got
some dancin' to do." And with that he whirled his girl
away as the band opened up.

Had Luther been sober Scott might have held him
there; had he been a white man he would have done the
same thing. As it was, common sense told him to keep his
patience and await another chance. It came a little later,
between encores, when another man came along to claim

Luther's partner. By the time Luther reached the bar, Scott was only a step behind. He moved in close and touched his mate's shoulder.

"Luther!"

He watched the man's head come round and saw the dull eyes try to focus. It was an effort but Luther made it.

"Mr. Scott," he said, straightening his shoulders as best he could. He grinned loosely and wiped his lips with the back of his hand. "What you doin' here?"

"Looking for you," Scott said. "I want to talk to you a minute."

"Yes, sir. Soon's I get my rum."

He waited as his order was placed in front of him and brought out a handful of bills and silver from which he found the proper change.

"I stopped by your house but your wife didn't know where you were so I tried a few bars," Scott said. "They told me at the Palmetto you might be here."

"That's right." Luther grinned. "Good place the Palmetto."

"They said something about your going to B. G."

"Might have said so."

"You meant Trinidad, didn't you?"

"B. G."

Scott was standing fairly close to Luther and he was conscious of the jostling as others tried to pass behind him. Now a man moved in between him and Luther, shouldering in such a way that Scott had to brace himself or step aside. He glanced up irritably and what he saw was a big man in a double-breasted jacket that was too wide in the shoulders and three inches too long. Under the straw hat the heavy, coarse-featured face seemed muscular rather than fat and the man's attention seemed centered on the bartender.

Scott felt himself forced aside by the weight of the other's body, so he stepped round and edged in on the other side of Luther.

"What's this about B. G?" he asked. "You mean British Guiana?"

"That's right."

"Why are you going there?"

"Got me a job."

"But look—"

Scott felt the tap on his shoulder before he could complete his thought. It was his friend in the double-breasted jacket. His black face was six inches from Scott's, the opaque eyes expressionless.

"Why don't you leave him alone?" he said softly.

Scott put down his rising anger. He did not understand much of this but there was something here he did not like. He hesitated, instinct telling him to take it easy.

"Let him have his good time," the other said, still softly.

"He works for me," Scott said. "I'm not bothering him."

"He ain't working tonight. Time's his own, ain't it?" He glanced at Luther who seemed oblivious to the conversation. "The man's drunk. He don't know what he doing."

Scott thought of all the things he could say if this had happened elsewhere but he said none of them. Instead he slid his hand inside Luther's upper arm and drew him firmly away from the bar.

"Come on, Luther," he said. "Let's go out where we can talk. Get some air."

Then, half expecting some argument he turned his back on the big man. There was no further trouble. Luther let himself be guided through the ring of on-lookers, and then they were circling the floor and head-ing for the open rear door. It took quite awhile but Scott was in no hurry and Luther did not seem to care so long as he could hang on to his drink of rum and water. They had a little trouble getting past the crush around the band but in another minute they were out-side and going down the steps to this fenced-in yard, deserted now with the music rocking.

By that time Scott had but one thought in mind: to get Luther away from here and into the car. He had no idea what lay behind Luther's change of heart and manner; he only knew that something had happened to change him. This morning—it seemed like a week ago—he had told Luther the cruise was to be postponed and the man had accepted the news without comment. Now—well, the thing to do was get him away from here and sober him up and make him talk.

And so Scott angled towards this gap in the fence which gave on the alley, talking softly, his inflection coaxing lest Luther decide to balk.

"When is it you're going to B. G., Luther?" he asked.

"With de tide."

"I thought you were working for me."

"Was. But this morning you say you don't need me."

"I said we were going to put the cruise off for a couple of days. I said I'd pay you anyway."

Luther did not reply to this. He stopped to empty his cup and then threw it from him, and now Scott was leading the way through the opening in the fence.

"Who gave you this new job, Luther?"

"Don't rightly know," Luther said, and then he staggered to a stop and stiffened in his tracks.

Scott still had a light hold on Luther's arm and now, without warning, he was bumped from one side. That told him that someone had been waiting for him and what happened then resolved itself in action that was silent, furious, and swiftly ended.

An unseen hand clamped on his shoulder and twisted him off balance. He let go of Luther's arm and instinctively struck the hand from his shoulder, turning now and seeing the vague outline of a man without knowing who he was. He thought first of the fellow who had interfered at the bar but the face beneath the hatbrim was as black as the night and the only thing he could be sure of was that the man had strength and bulk.

It also seemed clear that, whoever he was, he objected to Scott's tactics in questioning Luther, though Scott had no time to dwell on the assumption; for as he freed himself from the grasp he sensed the move that followed.

He did not see the fist but he diagnosed the body movement and stepped close, inside the blow, hammering in a hook to the body and slamming the other hand to the head. He connected with both. He heard the man grunt and saw him stagger back. Then, as he moved in, he heard the sound of sudden movement behind him and tried to turn as instinct warned him.

He did turn. He tried to duck away from this unseen threat, understanding now that there had been not one man waiting for him, but two. Then, his thoughts hanging there, he saw from the corner of his eye a blur of white close by. In that same instant something exploded against the back of his skull and the sky fell in on him.

15

THE FIRST thing that Alan Scott was aware of was the rhythmic throbbing of pain inside his head. It was a confused and disembodied sensation, distant and unreal, until he realized his eyes were open and the pain and the throbbing were unrelated. The pain came from inside his skull all right but the other was the enthusiastic beat of the orchestra and the stamp of dancing feet.

He lay on his back staring at the starred sky above him. When he dared try he sat up slowly, swallowing against the nausea that threatened to overwhelm him. Keeping his head back he breathed deeply until the sickness abated and then he rose slowly, half pushing himself erect to anchor himself on spread legs while he glanced round in the darkness.

The alley was empty all the way to the next street. Light spilled from the rear door and windows of the dance hall but the yard seemed as empty as the alley and now he went back through the fence, heading for the steps, touching the back of his head gingerly as he located the swelling beneath the hair and finding it sticky but not wet.

He climbed the steps with difficulty and stood a moment in the light of the open door. He straightened his jacket and felt his bow tie. The knees of his light gray slacks were stained but not torn and he wondered why his right hand was sore until he glanced down and saw the skinned knuckles.

Common sense told him that Luther was no longer about but he stepped inside nevertheless and began to circle the dancers, a lanky, somber-eyed figure with tousled brown hair and a lean angular face that was wet and shiny from the sickness that still bothered him. He was not aware of the curious glances this time for his mind was busy and his thoughts were centered elsewhere.

He kept looking for the man in the double-breasted jacket who had argued about Luther at the bar, hardly expecting to find him but taking his look just the same. He remembered how long it had taken him and Luther to reach the rear door. Plenty of time for anyone to have ducked out the front way and circled back into the alley. Positive now that there had been two men waiting, he was less sure about something else.

The impression remained that he *had* seen a white blur before he lost consciousness. From what? A white shirt—or a white face?

Esther Kane—if that was what her name was—was still presiding over the table in front of the entrance. She stopped talking to her companion of the moment when she saw Scott and he felt again the hostility of her stare. He went down the steps and the babble of conversation from the others on the porch followed him, foreign sounding and incoherent to his ears.

It gave him a forlorn and empty feeling as he paused at the edge of the paving. He could not have felt more alone had the language been Hottentot and it was hard to believe that this was a British colony and that such places as the Yacht Club and Aquatic Club could exist but a few miles away. Then, moving slowly out of the shadows diagonally across the street, he saw the blue-caped constable.

He was a tall, well-built Negro and he touched his cap as Scott approached. His voice was soft, educated, and easily understandable as he said good evening and asked if Scott had been enjoying the dance.

"I had a little trouble," Scott said.

"Trouble, sir?"

"Somebody jumped me."

"Jumped you?" The constable wrestled with the statement. "You mean, assaulted you?"

"Yeah."

"In the hall?"

"Out back. I came to look for a fellow who works for me. He was drunk and I took him out back to talk to him." Scott told the rest of the story in clipped resentful phrases and even as he spoke he began to realize that all this was a waste of time. The constable presently confirmed the idea.

"Could you identify this man?"

"Maybe."

The constable paused, his attitude suggesting he was reluctant to pursue the matter.

"If you wish," he said, "I will return with you. If you can pick this man out—"

"I doubt if he's still there."

"Then," said the constable with obvious relief, "it would be best for you to make a full report to the sergeant."

"What sergeant?"

"I will direct you to the sub-station," the constable said, and proceeded to do so.

Scott listened. He was about to turn away when a new thought occurred to him.

"Have you seen any other white man around here?"

"I saw you come when I was here before. I saw your car stop as I walked down the other side of the street. That is your car there," he said, pointing.

Scott nodded remembering how the two constables had separated at the corner.

"Just as you left," the man continued, "another car stopped some distance behind you, A white man was driving but"—he peered off into the night—"I do not see that car now."

"You didn't see anyone hanging around here?"

"I have just now returned, sir."

Scott found the district sub-station without difficulty. It was perhaps three quarters of a mile from the dance hall, a two-storied, rather new-looking building, with a low wall fronting on the road and a place to park between wall and entrance. Lights showed through the open windows on both floors and as Scott stopped the sedan he could see two men behind the long counter that seemed to bisect the lower, lefthand room.

He watched them a moment, his engine still running, and suddenly he knew that to make a complaint here under the circumstances would be pointless. Resentment and frustration had brought him here but now as his thoughts clarified he saw that the important thing was not that he find the man who fought with him; the one thing that mattered now was that he find Luther.

Luther had apparently acquired new wealth. Luther was going to British Guiana and someone seemed intent on making sure that he did. Who?

That was the question.

Luther himself had done nothing wrong. He was having himself a time but no charge could be brought against him, provided he was properly cleared to make this trip to British Guiana—

Scott shifted gears and swung the sedan back on the road, his mind elaborating possibilities as he drove back to the dance hall and made the turn which would take him back to Roebuck Street. Once there he continued on to Trafalgar Square, and now, seeing the bridge which crossed the *Careenage* and separated it from the inner basin, he stopped the car to consider again his alternatives.

What he saw as he sat there was quite different from the daytime picture he was accustomed to, for this was really the heart of the city with the municipal buildings at one side and the life line of the *Careenage* at the other. Normally the square was bustling with activity. Hawkers of both sexes sold fruits and vegetables, pottery, baskets, and sugar drinks; eagle-eyed taxi drivers from the nearby stand were loud and persistent in their solicitations and a continuous procession of buses loaded and unloaded at nearby corners.

Now the square was quiet. The surface of the inner basin was glassy and crowded with row after row of heavy, native-built lighters. There were no cars on the street which bordered the wharves, no trucks, no bicycles, no donkey carts; only the line of schooners which carried most of the inter-island trade, moored bow to stern, their spars spidery and indistinct against the night sky.

Scott turned in this direction, stopping the sedan opposite the first schooner. It looked deserted when he walked close to it and he continued on to the next one.

Here light showed from a hatch and under the awning
spread aft someone was singing softly to the accompani-
ment of a quatro. The strumming continued as Scott
stepped close, but something stirred in the thick shadows and presently a man appeared at the rail, a burly,
bare-armed fellow in tattered trousers.

"You want something, boss?"

"Do you know of any boat sailing to B. G. tonight or in
the morning?"

"Heard say the *Estelle* goin' to B. G."

"When's high tide?"

"Should be 'round four in de morning."

Scott thanked him and turned in the direction of the
roadstead, passing first a long, trim-looking craft that
looked like an old Nova Scotiaman. When he saw that
the decks were dark and deserted and the hatches tight
he continued on to the stern of the schooner moored
just ahead. Here there was some activity. He could not
see much but he heard voices and saw the lighted pilot
house and now, leaning close to the stern he saw the
name *Estelle,* and under that: Bridgetown, B.W.I.

With that he turned back towards the car, his mind
made up. The thing that had worried him most and had
brought him here on his own was the tide. He was not
sure just what he might have done had he found the
Estelle ready to sail, but now that there was time he had
no intention of sticking his neck out. Heretofore each
time he had done so someone had clipped him and now,
wanting help, he drove across the bridge and along
lower Bay Street until he came to the gray-walled enclosure which housed the Harbor Police.

He had passed it often but he had never been inside
and now, driving through the gate and parking, he saw

that there were several small buildings, reminding him somehow of the Central Police Station but on a smaller scale. Choosing the one which had the brightest lights he went up two steps and across a small porch to this bare-looking room where, behind a chest-high counter, two uniformed Negroes watched him approach. One sat near a small switchboard and the other, with sergeant's chevrons on his sleeve, got up from behind his desk.

"Yes, sir," he said.

Scott opened his mouth and then he closed it. Until now he'd had this idea in mind about finding Luther and making him talk. Something very wrong was happening and he had to know why. It had all seemed very simple until this instant when, his inner confusion mounting, he thought: *What the hell am I going to say?*

"I'm looking for a man named Luther," he said, aware that he had to start somewhere. "He works for me aboard the schooner *Griselda.*"

"Yes, sir." The sergeant nodded, waiting.

"He was at a dance tonight," Scott said and went on to explain briefly what had happened.

"I see," the sergeant said, though it was obvious that this was not so. "Someone assaulted you and you wish to make a complaint. But this should have been done in the district where the offense happened."

"I'm not interested in the assault," Scott said patiently. "I'm interested in finding Luther. He said something about going to British Guiana tonight."

"Yes, sir."

"He was drunk."

Scott hesitated, aware that he was not getting through to the sergeant who remained respectful but somewhat confused by the things he had heard.

"What is it you wish me to do?" he asked finally.

"I found out the schooner *Estelle* is sailing around four in the morning."

"Yes, sir." Still patient.

"I want to find out if Luther is aboard. I want to find out if—well, if his papers are in order. If the captain has him listed as a passenger."

He stopped again, his annoyance mounting, not at the sergeant but at himself. How could he explain what he wanted? What grounds did he have for demanding that the schooner be searched and that Luther, if found, be hauled ashore for questioning? He had the frustrated feeling that he could stand here all night and still not produce a good and sufficient reason for any action on the sergeant's part; what made it more galling was that it was his fault, not the sergeant's. For another second or two he waited, feeling the perspiration soaking his undershirt and running down his neck. Then, the stubborn slant of his bony jaw tightening, he leaned across the counter.

"Look," he said as calmly as he could. "Will you call Major Briggs for me?"

"Major Briggs, sir?" the sergeant was aghast. "At this hour?"

Scott glanced at the wall clock, a little amazed that it was only 11:20.

"I want to talk to him . . . If you don't want to call him," he said when the other hesitated, "give me his number and I'll call him—if you'll let me use the phone."

The sergeant remained unconvinced. "I don't know if—"

Scott cut him off. "If you don't want to cooperate I'll

go to a hotel and call him." He took a breath and tried again. "I own the *Griselda*."

"Yes, sir."

"Last night a woman was murdered aboard her."

"I heard a woman was found dead."

"All right. And Major Briggs is investigating that death. I think Luther knows something about it and I know damn well the Major should be told Luther is going to B. G. while there's still time. If you want to take the responsibility for—"

There was no need to finish the thought. The sergeant opened a gate in the counter and waved him towards a desk. He spoke to the constable at the switchboard and a minute later Scott heard the Major's voice.

"Briggs here."

"Alan Scott," Scott said and explained where he was. Then, as briefly as he could, he spoke about Luther. "I think he knows something about what happened last night and I think we ought to talk to him before he gets off the island. It might be important."

"I agree," Briggs said. "Give me about ten minutes. Now put the sergeant on again, will you?"

Scott stood up and nodded to the sergeant. He went through the gate and found a chair in the front part of the room. He heard the sergeant making other calls after he had hung up on Briggs but Scott paid little attention to what was said. He lit a cigarette, leaned back, and began to explore the sticky lump on the back of his head.

If Major Briggs felt any annoyance at having his evening at home interrupted he did not show it. His jacket

with its ribbons was immaculate as always, as were his
slacks which had been substituted for the day-time
shorts, and when he removed his cap his sandy hair was
smoothly combed. He returned the sergeant's salute per-
functorily but his attention remained on Scott as he
swung a chair close, dropped into it, and demanded details of the incident at the dance hall.

"Very well," he said when the account was finished,
"I think I have the picture." He nodded. He started to
rub his palms together but found it impractical. "What
I'm not quite clear on is why you wanted to talk to
Luther in the first place."

Scott swallowed. He was not in the best of moods and
he wanted no repetition of his conversation with the
sergeant so he made his reply as explicit as he could.

"I think Julia was murdered last night," he said flatly.
"Maybe you do too but you haven't admitted it. If I'm
right someone went out to the schooner last night, either
in a boat or by swimming."

"Swimming?" The Major's eyes opened wider. "I
hadn't considered that possibility."

Scott still remembered the wet spots on the deck but
because he did not want to go into that now, he stuck to
the subject of Luther.

"Luther lived close to the beach," he said. "He often
walked along it at night. He told me so before. Somebody in my dinghy—or one like it—made an attack on
Sally Reeves."

"That's what she says."

"Somebody was rowing about in a dinghy," Scott
said, ignoring the comment. "I wondered if Luther
might have seen something or somebody that would
substantiate my idea that someone *did* go out there to

kill Julia. I didn't seem to be getting much help from you on that angle so I thought it wouldn't hurt to ask Luther."

He took a breath and said: "Luther wasn't home. I went in four bars looking for him and missed him each time. But I found out that Luther had money and that he mentioned something about going to British Guiana. I went to that dance tonight to see him and you know what happened there. So now I'm trying to get the idea across to you, and I'll lay you three to one that I'm right, that Luther *did* see something. Why would he suddenly be going to British Guiana when he's working for me unless someone wanted to get him off the island? Where did he get the money? Why was someone at the dance keeping an eye on him?"

"You think you were attacked to prevent Luther from talking?"

"And to make sure he got aboard the *Estelle*."

Briggs glanced up as two uniformed constables entered along with a man in plain-clothes. When they came to attention he told them at ease and went over to the counter where he spoke to the sergeant and inspected a slip of paper which was handed to him.

"I'm inclined to agree with you," he said to Scott when he came back. "As a matter of fact we've had trouble before with the skipper of the *Estelle*. A few little things, minor infractions. Immigration tells the sergeant that there is no record of a man name of Luther listed either as a passenger or a member of the crew. So suppose we have a look. You can ride with me."

Major Briggs may have been slow to make up his mind about some things but once a decision was reached he acted with efficiency and dispatch. With Scott beside

him and the van-type truck with his three men following, he drove to the quayside and parked opposite the
Estelle.

After that the progression of this search and seizure
routine was a little confused for Scott, partly because it
was dark and partly because he could not understand
too much of what was being said. He stood on the after-
deck with Briggs while the three men got busy and in
no time at all the crew was lined up for Briggs' inspection. With a flashlight he examined the ship's papers and
then turned to Scott.

"The captain has not yet come aboard," he said, "but
the mate is here."

He focused his light on a husky Negro whose round
muscular face was familiar to Scott. Its owner was the
man who had interfered with his questioning of Luther;
at least that was Scott's impression. The natty double-
breasted jacket had been replaced by khaki trousers and
shirt and the fellow was now bareheaded but the face
was the same. When he stepped close and saw the bruise
on the hinge of the jaw he said this was the man who
had tangled with him in the alley.

"Ever see this gentleman before?" Briggs said, addressing the mate and indicating Scott.

"No, sir."

"Were you at a dance tonight?"

The mate hesitated and then apparently deciding that
others could place him at Esther Kane's party, he said:

"Yes, sir."

"All right. This is your complete crew?"

"Yes, sir."

"You don't know anything about a man named Luther?"

"No, sir."

"Well, we shall see," Briggs said, and gave an order to his two constables who disappeared down the lighted companionway.

On deck the minutes dragged and the lined-up crew stood motionless and almost invisible in the darkness. No one said anything and there was no sound but the gentle lapping of the water against the hull. When the constables reappeared they moved forward without a word, their progress measured by the beam of a flashlight until it vanished.

Another constable mounted on a bicycle appeared on his rounds and when he came to the rail to see what was going on Briggs ordered him aboard. Then, a minute or so later, the flashlight gleamed far forward and the two constables came aft carrying the limp body of a man which they placed carefully on deck while Briggs put the flashlight on his face.

"Is that the man?" he said to Scott.

Scott said yes and Briggs wasted no further time. He had the unconscious Luther carried to the van and told the plain-clothes man to take the mate in custody. Two constables were stationed on deck to make sure the *Estelle* did not sail and one was ordered to bring the captain to the Harbor Police Station when he came on board.

"The rest of you," he said, addressing the crew, "can carry on."

Scott did not see the mate again, once they returned to the station house. Someone led him from the van to one of the other buildings and Scott went along with Luther as he was carried to a cot in a small room at the rear of the office. Briggs had a doctor summoned and

while they were waiting he eyed Scott thoughtfully for
a long moment; then he smiled.

"Good man," he said.

"What?"

"This idea of yours about Luther. You didn't know if
he could tell us anything or not but you wanted to be
sure and so you tackled the job on your own. Appreciate
your cooperation. Shouldn't be a bit surprised if this fellow Luther could help us. I mean it would be damned
odd if all this was just some silly coincidence. At any
rate we'll have the captain and mate up before the magistrate in the morning."

It was a lot of talk for Briggs and for the first time
Scott began to feel that he had accomplished something
worthwhile. He was impatient to hear what Luther had
to say, and it pleased him to think that he had come to
Briggs for help instead of trying to bull things through
on his own.

He stood up when the doctor came but Briggs asked
him to wait so he sat down again while the two men
went into the back room. When they came out again
two minutes later Briggs was frowning.

"I'm afraid we'll have to wait until morning," he said.
"Unlikely that Luther will come round before then."

"Too drunk?"

"According to the doctor, he's been given a drug of
some kind." Briggs took Scott's arm and walked him to
the door. "Suppose you drop in at my office at—say, ten
in the morning if it's convenient. Unless I send word to
the contrary."

16

THE FEELING of elation and accomplishment that
had come to Alan Scott before he had heard the doctor's
verdict was gone before he reached his car. He slid in behind the wheel and sat motionless and brooding while
an odd restlessness began to warp his thoughts. He had
done a good job. Briggs had said so. Luther would talk
in the morning. When he had told his story they would
know who had hired him, so why not stop some place
and get the drink he needed so badly, and then go back
to the schooner?

That was the sensible thing to do and yet even as he
accepted the conclusion he knew he had to clear up just
one more point before he could go to sleep. For the impression lingered, though he had not said so to Briggs,
that the one who had struck him down from behind in
the alley was a white man. To bolster the impression
that this white blur he had seen so fleetingly was indeed
a face, he now added the argument that only a white
man with money would make this attempt to get Luther
off the island. And so, the impatience riding him anew,
he started the car and drove through the gateway, turning not to the right towards the Aquatic Club but to the
left towards the city.

What he planned to do was a very simple matter. He
was not sure just when he had been knocked out but
it must have been somewhere between ten thirty and
eleven. What could be easier then than to get this drink

he needed and at the same time check up on some of
his friends?

He had never been to the Surf Club but he knew its
general location, so once again he drove the length of
Broad Street, his mood improving as he rolled through
the deserted streets and came finally to Highway 1
which skirted the leeward coast. He had been once to
Paradise Beach for a drink so he had no trouble finding
his way, and presently he saw the lights of the club and
cottages down the hill to his left, beyond which the surf
broke whitely in long curling lines.

There were no buses now, and only an occasional car,
and with the hills behind him and the country flat as it
paralleled the coast, he cut his speed down so that he
would not miss the sign he was looking for. He found it a
little farther on and then he was bouncing down a
straight but narrow road towards a cluster of lights
which showed through the trees and came from the detached units that Howard Crane had once described as
well as the main building, a whitish, modern-looking
structure, two-storied in the center and having two one-
story wings extending at an angle.

There were a half dozen cars parked in the circular
drive and he got as close to the main entrance as he
could. Then he was moving through the foyer and seeing the broad covered room which was open at the far
side and overlooked the patio-like expanse beyond. The
furniture was modern and colorfully cushioned, and the
dozen or so guests who were having coffee and drinks
here glanced up to examine him idly as he stood there
to get his bearings.

Down the hall on the right and opening to the beach
much as the main room did was a dining room and now,

turning to his left he found the bar, one of the smallest he had ever seen. There were no stools, no rail, no customers. The customers, it seemed, did their drinking in more comfortable positions here at the Surf Club, but there was a barman so Scott ordered his drink and asked if Crane was around.

"Yes, sir," the man said. "At least he was." He turned to speak to a waiter who had come to give an order. "See if Mr. Howard's in the office."

Scott had just finished his drink and was pushing the glass forward for a refill when Crane came along the hall from the left. For a moment he looked surprised and then his tan, blunt-jawed face twisted in a grin and he quickened his step.

"Well," he said, "Hello. I thought you had an engagement."

"I got through earlier than I expected," Scott said. "Have the others gone?"

"About ten minutes ago. You probably passed them."

Scott nodded. He said he drove out on the chance that they might still be there. Crane said he was sorry and Scott said it was all right, he needed the drink anyway and besides he'd never been out here before.

"It's very attractive," he said.

"It is rather." Crane signed Scott's check and took him by the arm. "Bring your drink," he said. "You can't see much at night but let's step out front a minute."

Scott went along through the front room to the terrace beyond with its white chairs and glass-topped tables. He could not see the water but Crane said it was fifty yards ahead through the trees.

"Marvelous beach," he said in his "Bajan" accent. "No sea eggs. Hardly ever any surf." He chuckled. "Still it's a good name for a club, don't you think? Surf Club. Has a nice connotation."

He pointed out other features of the place and Scott let him go, making the proper comments when called for. When he had a chance he said:

"Did they all go back together? The Farrows and—"

"Yes," Crane said, and then reconsidered. "That is, the Farrows and Sally Reeves and Freddie went back in the Farrows' car just awhile ago. I stayed on for a bit to go over some things with my manager but Keith went back earlier. Right after dinner as a matter of fact."

"Oh?"

"Said he had a headache, though I imagine that was only an excuse."

"When was that?"

"It might have been around ten. Keith wasn't very good company tonight. You remember how he was at the Farrows'? Edgy. Out of sorts. Hardly blame him though. He's had to see about shipping the body back to the States and trying to locate some relative of Julia's and—"

He broke off and they walked back into the building and Scott said he had better be on his way.

"Have another one of those before you go," Crane said, tapping Scott's glass.

"No, thanks. These two were just what I needed."

"Well—all right. But do come up some time when it's daylight. Some afternoon. I'd like to show you what we have here. Bring your swim things." He grinned. "Bring Sally."

Scott said it sounded like a good idea and he would consult Miss Reeves, knowing as he spoke—as Crane must also have known—that this was only small talk and that no one was going to have any fun until Julia's death had been properly explained.

The Aquatic Club bar and concessions had been closed for the night when Scott parked his car at the Yacht Club and came out on the beach. A light showed here and there but he saw no one, and as he stood there by his dinghy he found himself wondering if Sally had gone to bed. He did not want to disturb her, but if there was a light on in her apartment—

He made no attempt to rationalize the impulse that started him along the beach. He was not at the moment worried about her; he simply wanted to hear her voice and see her smile again. What he might say if he had the opportunity did not concern him as he hurried along, cutting now to his left through the trees so he could skirt the end of the pier.

There were a few cars in the parking lot, apparently belonging to tenants of this row of small apartments where Sally was staying, and he was still some distance away when he realized that of the second-floor apartments, one showed light through the tilted shutters and this one was Sally's. Then, even as he watched it, he saw the door open and close, saw the shadowy figure start along the gallery towards the stairs at the end.

Scott did not know who it was, nor did he understand why anyone should be coming from her room at this hour. This in itself was enough to make him quicken his steps. For the strain was working on him and had been for many hours, though he may not have realized it, and his nerves were jumpy, his thoughts apprehensive rather than practical.

His chief concern was, and always had been, Sally;

and now, slipping into the thick shadows below the gallery, it seemed important that he know who had been with her—and why.

He could hear the steps coming down now as he waited beneath the outside stairs and, still not knowing who it was, he stepped into the open so that this man, who had turned towards the parking lot, bumped into him. He heard the startled gasp as the man stiffened and then he was looking down into the round bespectacled face of Freddie Gardner.

"Hello, Freddie."

"Oh—" Freddie exhaled noisily. "You—you startled me."

"Kind of late to be calling, isn't it?"

"Calling? I brought her home."

"What?"

"My car was at Howard's. The Farrows drove us up there and I brought Sally home. Keith had left earlier."

Simple enough. A reasonable explanation. That is what Scott's sense of logic told him. His emotions, however, were less tractable. For in the back of his mind were the thoughts of Julia lying dead in the forward cabin, of the attack on Sally by someone in the dinghy, the plan to get Luther off the island. All these things served to point up Scott's own fears and what he did then was perhaps more impulsive than well reasoned, and, having made up his mind, he stuck stubbornly to the decision.

"Is everything all right?" he asked.

"Why—yes, naturally."

"Let's go back up and see."

"What?" Freddie peered up at him through the darkness.

"I just want to be sure."

"Don't be a damned fool. I brought her home. I went in for a minute."

"Come on." Scott's grip tightened on the other's arm. "It won't take long."

"No." Freddie tried to jerk free but Scott caught his sleeve. "Will you stop this damned nonsense."

"Come on," Scott said, still grimly patient. "Humor me."

Freddie tried again and now Scott had a wristlock on him and so they turned and marched up the steps and along the gallery, Freddie muttering under his breath but no longer resisting. Sally answered Scott's knock almost immediately.

"Yes?" she said.

Scott identified himself and the door opened. With the light behind her he could not see her face but she apparently had been combing her hair since it slanted over one eye and she was still fully dressed.

"What is it?" She looked from one to the other. "Is something wrong?"

"No," Scott said and let go of Freddie. "My mistake, pal," he said wearily. "I must have had what you fellows call the wind up."

Freddie grunted. His muffled remark sounded profane but was otherwise unidentifiable. He shrugged his drill jacket in place and stalked indignantly towards the stairs.

Sally was still puzzled. "What happened?"

"One of my screwy ideas," Scott said, drawing her out on the gallery and reaching behind her to close the door.

Over in the parking lot a car's headlights slashed through the trees. A motor started and the car came briefly in view as it circled. That was how Scott happened to see the cracked lens that he had seen twice before, once that night and once the night before.

"What?" he said, aware that Sally had spoken.

"Would you please," she said with dry good humor, "tell me what this is all about?"

"Yes," said Scott, and he did, feeling more like a fool with each word he spoke. Sally did not help his mood any when she chuckled.

"Freddie?" she said. "You thought Freddie might—"

"Somebody killed Julia," he cut in doggedly. "How do you know it wasn't Freddie? Somebody tried to brain you with an oar. You say you don't know who it was."

"But I don't."

"The point is, does the guy know this? Maybe he thinks you're holding back because you don't want to put the finger on him. How does he know you might not change your mind?"

"Pooh. That's silly."

"Okay. So I'm a silly guy. I saw someone come out of here and I didn't know who it was, and when I found out I still had to be sure you were all right. I couldn't go to sleep until I knew."

He said all this quickly and when he ran out of breath he reached out and caught her arms. Before she knew what was happening he had pulled her close and kissed her soundly, a thing he had wanted to do for a long time. It was not an expert kiss nor a passionate one, but he found it highly satisfactory and now, not waiting for her reaction he stepped back and started to turn away. Then he stopped.

It was too dark to see her face or to know what she

thought. He thought he saw the soft curve of her smile but when she remained silent he said:

"I'll go quietly if you'll tell me why Freddie came in?"

"He said he wanted to talk to me a minute."

"He drove you home. He had plenty of time to talk."

"He had the time but he didn't. He hardly said a word. He seemed very unlike Freddie tonight."

"And Lambert was unlike Lambert tonight."

"Yes, he was."

"So what did Freddie want to talk about?"

"Well"—she hesitated, her voice thoughtful—"he sort of hemmed and hawed. He couldn't seem to get started. It was almost as if he had come to say something else and then changed his mind. That was my impression but what he actually did was apologize for telling Major Briggs about the pillow. He said he hadn't realized it would make it difficult for me. He knew I hadn't had anything to do with Julia's death and he was sorry if he involved me in any way."

"All right." Scott opened the door for her and waited until she was inside. He studied her a moment, half closing one eye. "About that kiss," he said. "That's just a starter. There'll be more. The best way to avoid them is to keep out of my way."

She looked right back at him, amused glints in her green eyes. "Thanks for the warning," she said. "I'll keep it in mind."

"And another thing," Scott said, gruff now. "That door was unlocked when I knocked. Lock it. I'll wait."

He pulled the door shut. When he heard the key click he started quietly along the gallery, feeling very

pleased that he had come and the incident with Freddie
forgotten.

17

AT TEN o'clock the following morning Major Briggs sat
behind his desk rubbing his palms gently together and
feeling rather pleased with himself. In the preceding
hour he had managed to get a complete and reasonably
satisfactory statement from Luther and now, as an aide
announced Alan Scott, he was quite ready to pass along
the information that progress was being made.

When the door opened he watched his visitor cross
the room, answering his good morning and taking in the
rubber-soled shoes, the white duck trousers, and cord
coat. The blue eyes were steady and direct in the newly
tanned face and that made him wonder why it was that
Americans always made such a fetish of getting the
greatest possible tan out of the least possible time. He
admitted that it gave Scott a look of health and vigour
but all this had actually been there before; it showed
in the way the man moved and carried himself.

Now that the case was beginning to take on a likely
pattern he was also ready to admit that he liked this
young man and the way he conducted himself. It was
one of his jobs as a police officer to be suspicious of
people when suspicion was warranted and it was not
always too difficult to know when a person was lying.
It was the same with character, though this took more
time, and while he had believed in the beginning that

Scott had lied, he had not long considered him as a murder suspect. What he did not quite understand was why Scott had lied, but that was a thing he hoped to answer shortly.

"Yes," he said now in answer to Scott's question. "Our friend Luther talked quite nicely considering how he must have felt. He still looked somewhat seedy from the effects of that drug—whatever it was—but before I tell what he had to say I'd like to ask a few questions."

He paused as Scott settled back and crossed his legs, having his full attention now and wondering how best to phrase his question.

"Suppose I start," he said, "by asking if at any time you felt that you were under serious suspicion in this matter of Julia Parks' death?"

"No," Scott said.

"An innocent person seldom does unless circumstantial evidence becomes strong enough to scare him. In spite of what you say, you lied to us." He waited for some denial; when none came he continued:

"Now in this business we learn early that when an intelligent person lies to us we can very quickly get the truth, provided we keep him lying until we can trip him up and point out an inconsistency or two. The reason is that, confronted with inconsistencies, the intelligent person admits them, and having admitted them seems to realize the futility of further argument. A stupid man, on the other hand, will admit no inconsistency. If he makes up his mind to say he was home in bed at such and such a time, he will continue to say so no matter how many witnesses swear he was somewhere else."

He paused again, rubbing his palms together until he

realized he was doing it and recalled his wife's objec-
tion to the mannerism. What was it she said? That it
made him look smug and complacent, and altogether
too superior? He must watch it in the future.

"This was so in your case. You lied, but confronted
with the evidence of the hotel watchman, you changed
your story and told the truth—or at least most of it. You
were innocent and you lied. You went to the hotel room
and searched it. You persisted in certain other investigations of your own, fortunately for us, I might add, in
the case of Luther last night. I would be interested to
know why."

"Why what?"

"Why you involved yourself. Surely it was not just
curiosity. You're not a detective. You have no police
experience. Or have you?"

"No."

"You're not an attorney."

"I'm in the advertising business."

"Then why—"

"I'll tell you." Scott sat up and uncrossed his legs. His
smile was fixed but his gaze was untouched by that smile
and to Briggs there was neither truculence nor defiance
in the voice as it continued: "I was worried about Miss
Reeves."

"Ah," said Briggs. "I wondered about that."

"I knew about the pillow she tossed over Julia's face.
When I found her dead I went to Miss Reeves and told
her not to say anything to you. I was afraid you'd jump
to conclusions. I thought you might think it was an accident and blame her."

"You didn't think it was accidental."

"I thought it was murder but I couldn't prove it. I went to the hotel when I saw my chance because I hoped to find something that might give me some clue as to who was responsible."

"Apparently you didn't trust us to do the same thing in an official way."

He saw the grin come then, reluctantly it seemed, and somewhat sheepish. He saw the empty gesture of the hands and heard Scott say:

"Let's say I was worried and upset and not very smart. It was a silly thing to do; I admit it. I got this crazy idea and I followed it up."

Briggs nodded, understanding now the reasons for Scott's actions. "You're quite attached to Miss Reeves?"

"Yes, I am."

"Perhaps you're in love with her."

"Perhaps."

"You didn't want her to be blamed for Julia Parks' death. You weren't satisfied with the progress we were making so you conducted these investigations of your own, not so much to find out who was guilty—in case it was murder—but to prove it was indeed murder."

"I guess that's about it."

"Good." Briggs smiled. "Now I can relieve your mind." He hesitated seeing Scott lean forward expectantly. "That was a good show you put on last night with Luther. Helped us tremendously so I think it's only fair to tell you that we know Julia Parks was murdered."

"When did you find out?"

"Yesterday afternoon."

"Then why didn't you say so last night?"

"It didn't occur to me." Briggs chuckled. "You may

remember that we were otherwise occupied at the time. We had a full report from the surgeon shortly after you left here yesterday afternoon."

"And what convinced you?"

"Those stains on the pillow you noticed." Briggs slid his elbows across the desk, his gaze intent on Scott's angular face. "There was a smear or two of lipstick, as you suspected. But the larger stain was something else. Chemical analysis proved it."

"Oh." Scott swallowed. He scowled a silent moment; then his eyes opened. "Blood?"

"It seems," said Briggs, "that our murderer didn't realize that very little pressure would be needed to suffocate a person who is unconscious and helpless as Miss Parks was. The very weight of the pillow, if it were large enough, might be sufficient. But, not knowing this, we think our man put his weight on the pillow. The pillow over her face, his hand or fist in the center of the pillow and over her mouth and nose, and his weight on his hand."

He leaned back and said: "There was a tiny laceration on the inside of the woman's upper lip. The lip must have been pulled over her teeth by the movement of the pillow. The pressure cut it."

He watched the look of relief pass over Scott's face as the muscles relaxed, and now a smile grew there, the teeth flashing white.

"Then that eliminates Sally."

"It would seem so." Briggs picked up some papers on his desk and his manner was at once businesslike. "About our friend Luther," he began.

"Yeah," Scott said quickly. "Did he say who hired him?"

"Waldron."

Scott's gaze slid past Briggs to fix on some point outside the window, and if he felt any surprise he did not show it. "Waldron knew Julia had passed out on the schooner."

Then he was telling a story Briggs had not heard before, explaining how he had met Waldron the night Julia died, how he and Morgan and Waldron had discussed the woman and the *Griselda*, how Waldron had left shortly after Keith Lambert arrived.

"How much longer did you and Lambert stay?"

"I'd say a half hour at least."

"Time enough."

"Have you talked to him yet?"

"I'm about to pay him a call." Briggs reached for his cap and stick. "Come along if you like. You can ride with me and I'll have a man drive your car. I expect you'd like to know what Luther had to say."

Scott felt strangely weary as he leaned back against the cushions of the Major's car, but it was a physical weariness and could not diminish the warm, inner exultancy that had come with his thoughts of Sally. He was glad now that he had done the things he had, gladder still that all that was behind him. What happened now was police business and no concern of his, for with Sally in the clear he was through, finished, done.

He was still curious about Luther and Waldron but he understood that Briggs would tell him in good time, so he slumped down in his seat and watched the passing scene as Briggs turned on Broad Street and headed for Chamberlin Bridge. Crossing this he glanced seaward and discovered three ships anchored in the bay. One

was a Harrison Line freighter, the second a neat, trim-
looking passenger-cargo ship of the Canadian National
line, its white hull and superstructure glistening in the
morning sunlight; the one on the left was the French
liner *Colombie*, also white, in for the day from Havre by
way of Southampton and Martinique before continuing
southward. A few minutes later as they skirted the es-
planade, Briggs began to talk.

"I think Luther told the truth," he said. "It's not hard
to tell with that sort and I doubt if he had enough re-
sistance or originality this morning to think up this
particular story. You were right about his seeing
Waldron. The hour of day or night matters very little
to these people so he can't be sure of the time but he
did see Waldron come ashore in a skiff the night of the
murder. More important, Waldron saw him."

He braked sharply to avoid a donkey cart and said:
"According to Luther, Waldron told him that he had
borrowed the skiff which had been tied up at the landing stage of the Aquatic Club pier. He did not say where
he had been but he asked Luther to row the skiff back
where he—Waldron—got it. He gave Luther a bill—Luther did not look at it until later—and asked him to say
nothing about the skiff or having seen Waldron. He also
asked where Luther lived . . . Well, Luther did as directed. No one noticed him and when he found Waldron
had given him a ten-dollar bill he was ready to cooperate
further."

"Then," Scott said, "the next morning I told Luther
we wouldn't be taking the cruise for a few days."

"Exactly. And remember, Luther knew nothing about
any murder. There was nothing in yesterday's *Advocate*
about it. So when Waldron drove up yesterday morning

with a bottle of rum in his car, Luther was ready to listen."

"Waldron had a proposition."

"And one that would appeal to Luther. He told Luther he was in the market for a boat. He wanted Luther to go to British Guiana and see if he could locate a small sloop that would be a good buy for Waldron. It was quite a long story the way Luther told it but what it amounted to was that Waldron wanted a sloop. Luther knew boats. He was to try to find one in British Guiana and failing there, to try Port of Spain. To make the story more convincing Waldron gave Luther a fifty-dollar advance and the promise of a job as skipper of the sloop if Luther found one. The important thing was that Luther arrange passage yesterday if possible on whatever schooner might be heading south. He was to meet Luther that afternoon and pay for the passage etcetera, etcetera."

"All this was before you had Waldron down to your office."

"Exactly. We had not yet brought Waldron into the case but he was afraid we might and he was already making plans for Luther, the only person who knew where Waldron was the night before. Well, Luther found the *Estelle* was sailing early this morning—the information I got from the immigration man last night was wrong; Luther was listed as a passenger and had clearance but he was down not as Luther but as L. Lyman, his right name. Beyond that all Luther knows is that Waldron paid for the passage and that he—Luther —began touring the bars. He remembers going to the dance but that's all. He doesn't recall seeing you or know how he got aboard the *Estelle*."

Scott thought it over, understanding how all this could happen when a man like Waldron was behind it. "Waldron must have got to that mate somehow."

"It would seem so," Briggs said. "Probably hired the mate to make sure Luther was aboard."

"What's the mate say?"

"Nothing. Pleads ignorance of the whole business. We're questioning the crew but don't expect much in that direction either."

"I think Waldron came to that dance too," Scott said.

"Might well have. The mate locates Luther, sees he's drunk and phones Waldron for further directions."

Scott was ready to accept the premise when he remembered the telephone which rang as he was leaving Waldron's place the night before, but before he had a chance to comment on this Briggs swung the car off the highway and came to a stop behind the bungalow.

"Well, here we are," he said, and waited for the plain-clothes C.I.D. man to bring Scott's car alongside.

When the man got out Briggs, whistling softly and rapping his calf with his swagger stick, led the way round the bungalow and up the steps of the front veranda overlooking the beach. He knocked three times, said: "Hmm," and tried the knob. When the latch clicked he stepped inside, glanced round, then continued on into the room.

While the plain-clothes man closed the door and stood beside it to await further orders, Briggs went on into the bedroom with Scott at his heels. He glanced in at the bath and, still whistling softly, came back to the front room to have a look at the kitchen. Back in the bedroom once more he stooped down to pick up a metal wastebasket. He stopped whistling and showed Scott the charred paper fragments which had apparently been burned in the basket.

"It looks," he said with startling unconcern, "as though our bird has flown his coop."

Scott opened the wardrobe. Suits and slacks still hung there but not as many as the night before, and the two bags were gone. He spoke of this as Briggs went through the drawers in the chest and did the same thing with the vanity.

"Gone all right," Briggs said. "A futile bit of business too, if you ask me. I'm afraid he'll find it a bit difficult getting off the island."

"He's had since last night," Scott reminded him.

"True." Briggs thought it over. "I suppose it's possible but we shall soon see."

He stepped to the telephone, dialed a number. When he had his connection he started the official wheels moving with a series of instructions and requests for reports. Scott moved to the native-built desk and opened the two vertical doors on either side. He had glanced through the inner shelves the night before and now he began to examine them with more care. Briggs, seeing what he was doing, spoke to the plain-clothes man.

"Lend a hand, sergeant. See what you can find of interest."

The man hunkered down in front of one door and began to remove papers and clippings from the shelves, glancing at each one before putting it aside. Scott was doing the same and what he found was a pile of receipted bills from local merchants, tear sheets from the *Advocate* of articles that had interested Waldron, a road

map of the island, programs from race meetings. He had
not quite finished when the telephone rang and Briggs
relayed his first report.

"There was a plane departure for San Juan and one
for Trinidad this morning," he said, "but both were
booked solid days in advance and there were no cancel-
lations. A schooner for St. Vincent and a sloop for St.
Lucia. If he's aboard we can have him taken off on arrival."

"Is this anything, sir?"

The sergeant had unfolded a sheet from a newspaper
and now he spread it on the desk as Briggs came close.
Scott stepped up beside him, seeing now that the page
came from the Sunday magazine section of a New York
daily. The three things he noticed first were the picture,
the penciled message scrawled across the top, and the
heading which read: WHAT HAPPENED TO TIM
WELSH? The sub-head continued: *Gambler Vanished
Without Trace 18 Months Ago.*

The article, date-lined ten days previous, had to do
with a much publicized case that Scott remembered as
he read on. It had started nearly two years ago with
the Grand Jury indictment of a man named Antonelle,
his partner, Tim Welsh, and a half dozen lesser lights
in connection with a bookmaking syndicate that eventually involved certain politicians and members of the
police department. For weeks the papers had been filled
with the developments and this article was a recapitula-
tion of that case, pointing up the results of the trials
which sent Antonelle and several others to prison but
featuring the mystery of Tim Welsh, who had jumped
bail and vanished with an estimated $200,000 of part-
nership cash.

The photograph of a fleshy-faced man with thinning hair and deep-set eyes seemed familiar but told Scott nothing at first glance; Briggs, with his policeman's gift of observation, thought otherwise.

"Thin down that face and tan it up," he said; "add a mustache and dark-rimmed glasses and I think we'll have our friend Waldron." He cocked his head. "Waldron—Welsh. Not very inventive in that respect, would you say. And what do you make of this?"

His finger underlined the penciled words on top which read: *"Didn't know you were so famous. Will be down soon to collect my share . . . J.*

"J for Julia, do you imagine?" Briggs said. "A comparative analysis of her handwriting should clear that up for us in any event."

"She must have recognized him when she saw this article," Scott said. "Or thought she did and took a chance."

"Mailed this down in advance to suggest that she would like some payment for her silence," Briggs added thoughtfully. "He tucked it in here with his other newspaper clippings and forgot where he put it, if he thought about it at all in his haste to get out." He folded the sheet and tapped it idly against one palm. "Interesting," he said. "Could make a first rate motive for murder."

18

WHEN Alan Scott awoke on his bunk it was nearly dark and he was so drugged with sleep that it took him a

while to understand how he happened to be here. He
had left Briggs and come to the Aquatic Club for a sandwich and a beer and then gone to Sally's place at two
o'clock only to find her gone. His lack of sleep during
the past forty-eight hours was finally getting the best of
him and when he came aboard he had flopped down to
take a small nap. Now, glancing at his watch, he saw
that it was a quarter of six and he sat up, his mouth
thick and his body moist from the heat of the little cabin.

Yawning, he got a cigarette going and sat for a moment scratching his head. It took an effort to peel off his
shorts and get into his trunks but when he went on deck
the soft breeze began to revive him and he sat down on
the cabin house to cool off before his swim.

As always it was the time of day he most enjoyed
and it was enough for the moment to watch the texture
of the waning sunlight on the water. There was activity
on the club pier now. The sound of music came to him
from some distant record player and up by the Need-
ham's Point Lighthouse the color of the sea changed
from blue to green before it broke upon the coral shoals.
It did him good, just sitting there with his cigarette. Life
seemed less complicated. The cruise no longer seemed
so important now that Lambert was going to buy the
Griselda, and the establishment of Sally's innocence was
like a great weight lifted from his shoulders.

He flipped the cigarette butt over the side and followed it into the water with a long, flat dive. Leisurely
he swam round the *Griselda's* counter, admiring her
lines, happy that for another three weeks she would be
his. Just as leisurely he pulled himself aboard and went
below to shower and dress. He made himself a small
drink, drank it with great enjoyment and, at a quarter of

seven, rowed over to the Aquatic Club pier for a second drink. It was here that Freddie Gardner found him.

Scott greeted him without enthusiasm. For some unknown reason Freddie made him think of murder, a subject he had been trying hard to forget, and somehow he found the other's somewhat shabby appearance distasteful. His offer of a drink was accepted and Freddie sidled into a chair and smoothed down his sandy hair.

"I hoped I'd find you here," he said. "I'd like your advice on something if you have a minute . . . It's about the other night," he said when he tasted his drink. "I suppose it's a moral problem, or an ethical one. What I mean to say is, Julia's death, tragic as it was, solved some problems for a lot of people."

"It didn't solve any problems for me," Scott said. "It loused up my cruise charter for God knows how long. I guess Lambert is going to buy the *Griselda* but—"

"True enough in your case," Freddie interrupted. "But for others it is somewhat different and I have a question I would like to ask." He leaned forward, lowering his voice. "If you knew who might have killed Julia would you say so?"

For a moment Scott could only stare at him, an odd irritation beginning to work on him. "But I don't know," he said. "For all I know, you did . . . All I know for sure is, I didn't, and neither did Sally Reeves."

"Sally went swimming that night."

The digression startled Scott. In spite of himself he remembered again the wet spots on the schooner's deck when he had gone below to find Julia's body. Then, because the inference was so monstrous, he closed his mind on the subject.

"Certainly she went in swimming," he said, infuriated that this little man should bring the matter up. "She said so."

"She said there was a man in a dinghy."

"She didn't say it was a man."

Freddie shrugged. "You're quibbling."

"So I'm quibbling. She saw someone in a boat. Someone tried to brain her. Maybe it was you—or maybe you know who it was."

Gardner removed his glasses and started to polish them on a none too clean handkerchief.

"Suppose I did."

"Suppose hell," Scott said. "You either did or you didn't, and if you didn't why bring the subject up? What is this, another chisel of yours?"

With his glasses off Freddie's gaze had a squint-eyed quality and a flush crept into his round face.

"Not at all," he said. "I just thought—"

"You thought," Scott interrupted, his anger still riding him. He started to amplify the reply and then, suddenly, he stopped. Having it in mind to accuse Freddie of hanging around the beach the night Julia died, he now recalled again the oddly broken headlight he had seen in Freddie's little car the night before. There had been something familiar about that broken lens but he had not been able to recall where he had seen it earlier. Now, in some mysterious and unaccountable way, his mind supplied the answer and he was sure.

He had seen it the night he had brought Lambert back from the Club Morgan. He had been turning into the Yacht Club and this car had suddenly appeared before him, coming either from the Yacht Club or some place close by. That had been somewhere around one o'clock and because he realized that Julia might have been dead even then—the medical report had never placed the time of death accurately—he spoke of this to Freddie, his voice curt and incisive, the reaction in the other's face telling him he was right.

"You didn't go home that night like you said you did," he said, "or if you did you came back later to sneak around in your own peculiar way. I guess you haven't told Major Briggs about that, have you?"

"No," Freddie said quietly. "I haven't. That's why—"

"Then why bother me? I'm no cop and I've got no dough to pay for information. Tell Briggs, Freddie. If you don't, I will . . . Now if you'll excuse me I'd like to order dinner."

Freddie rose without a word, his face still flushed and his bespectacled gaze evasive. He rearranged his chair and walked swiftly from the pier, a small, stooped figure in a rumpled white suit that had seen better days. Watching him go, remembering the things he had said, Scott felt the anger ooze away and presently there came to replace it the first prodding fingers of shame. He remembered Freddie's ever-ready laughter and its peculiar giggle-like quality. Freddie wasn't giggling any more. No one had laughed since Julia came and now, the depression settling upon him, Scott was no longer hungry. When the waiter came he asked if he could get a cup of soup and a sandwich served out here.

After that he began to think, not wanting to but unable to help himself now that Freddie had brought up again the subject of murder. His angular face was somber and his gaze remote as he began to rearrange the facts he knew and tried to find some pattern that he could accept. In the beginning he had been concerned with his own selfish problems of the cruise, the sale of the schooner; he had been jealous because he was in love, and unfair in that jealousy. He had been worried about Sally, and the things he had done, the lies he had told, had been motivated by that worry.

Now that worry came back to him, its basis the fact that Sally had probably seen the one who had killed Julia. He believed Sally when she said she did not know who that someone was but suppose there was something else, something she had not spoken of because she felt it unimportant. Was this recent business with Freddie some trick on his part to find out if Sally had told him—Scott—anything she had not told the police?

"Nuts!" he said, half aloud, annoyed that he should consider such far-fetched possibilities. What kind of thinking was that?

With an effort he brought his mind back to details he could be sure of, and out of them came one certain conclusion: he had acted foolishly in attacking Gardner instead of playing along and finding out how much he knew. Instead of temper he would have been better off displaying a little finesse.

By the time he had finished eating the worry was still there and he knew finally that he must find Freddie and do what he could to learn what it was Freddie had wanted to say. But first he wanted to see Sally and reassure himself that she was all right, to make sure once and for all that she had no knowledge that might prove dangerous.

It was dark when he climbed the outside stairs and went along the railed gallery to Sally's room. He knocked three times and tried the door before admitting that she was not there, and now, an odd uncertainty working on him, he went to the parking lot and found the attendant.

Yes, he knew Miss Reeves. He'd seen her leave about ten or fifteen minutes ago. "I don't rightly know where she went, sir. But you know Mr. Howard Crane? Well, he came to pick her up."

"Crane?"

Scott stood a moment, his face bleak and his gaze fixed and sightless in the darkness as he considered the information. When he could find no sinister implication in the statement he started to turn away; then he thought of something else.

"Do you know Mr. Gardner?"

"Mr. Freddie Gardner? Yes, sir."

"Could you tell me where he lives?"

"Could try, sir. You turn right out here," he said, pointing. "You go along the highway to—you know where the Baldwin Hotel is? Well, you pass that. I think it's the next gap," he said, using the local synonym for a secondary street. "Turn left. It should be marked; should say Dodd."

"Dodd Street?"

"Dodd's Gap. Mr. Gardner, he live in the last house."

Scott thanked him and gave him a coin. Then, leaving the dinghy tied up at the pier, he went along to the Yacht Club and his car.

Dodd's Gap was paved but narrow and the small houses which flanked it—some stone and some frame— stood on narrow plots and were separated from each other by walls or vine-covered fences. A half dozen cars were parked on one side, all facing the highway, and as Scott drove past he knew why: the street ended in a field with a turn-around and the residents apparently made the turn and headed properly before parking. Scott did the same, taking the first vacant space and then walking back to this frame house, standing well off the ground and having an unpainted, rundown look even in the darkness.

Yellow light rimmed the shades in the front room and Scott crossed a sandy yard. In a neighboring plot a dog was yapping and somewhere a radio was playing softly as he climbed the steps and moved across the veranda to the wooden door. He knocked, knocked again. When there was no answer he tried to peer round the shades. Finally he came back and tried the knob which turned easily enough.

At first he only opened the door about a foot, calling ahead of him. "Freddie! . . . Is anyone home?"

He widened the opening to take a forward step. Then he stopped, hand still on the knob, his stare suddenly wide and fixed, only vaguely aware of the sparsely furnished room with its washed-board floors but knowing now why Freddie Gardner had not answered his knock. Freddie lay crumpled on the floor, face down and one arm outflung.

Scott did not remember closing the door. He was conscious only of the still figure in the wrinkled white trousers and the short-sleeved shirt. Somehow he was on one knee beside it, his nerves stretched tight and his throat dry.

"Freddie!" he said again and put his hand on a shoulder that was limp and inert in his grasp. He shook it. He pulled at it, not meaning to, and the torso tipped over on its back and then he saw the ugly dark stain on the shirt front and the tiny little hole just to the left of the breastbone.

Until then Scott reacted without conscious thought. Now he lifted a limp wrist and sought a pulse-beat that never came. When he replaced the hand the sickness came and he forced his glance upward and away from the round face, pale now but composed, the eyelids closed in death.

19

IT WAS not the fact of death as such that held Scott there on one knee as reaction began its work; it was the thought of what he had said earlier, the fancied picture he had of Freddie shuffling off alone across the Aquatic Club pier to his death, because he, Scott, had been abusive and had refused to listen when Freddie asked for advice. There was no trick on Freddie's part. He had wanted help, needed help. He had known then who had killed Julia; he must have known. He had held back the information for some personal reason of his own, knowing this was wrong and bothered by the knowledge. Now—

With tremendous mental effort Scott forced the picture from his mind and tried to think. Still on one knee he let his harried glance move on, taking in the canvas chair, the cot with its bleached-blue covering, the table with the radio, the smaller one with the telephone. To his left was a darkened hall leading to other rooms, the door on one side of which stood ajar.

As remembered things came flooding back the pattern he had been seeking seemed to fall in place. He seemed to understand what had happened, and why. That it was nothing he could prove seemed unimportant now. He would tell what he knew and the rest would be up to Major Briggs.

When his glance came back to the telephone he knew what he had to do. He rose wearily. He took a breath but he did not touch the telephone or even make a move in that direction, then or ever.

It was luck rather than any great alertness or instinctive pressure on his part that warned him in time. One moment he was concerned only with the problem of murder and its ramifications; the next he stiffened as he stood, scalp tightening as a curious fear that was akin to panic took hold of him.

He had heard nothing at all but the distant radio. What he had seen was but a shadow of movement, caught briefly in the corner of his eye.

The door in the hallway which stood ajar had moved.

Not much. No more than an inch. Except for the acuteness of his vision he would not have noticed it at all.

He did not try to tell himself this was nothing but pressure of ragged nerves on imagination. *The door had moved.* Someone was waiting in the darkness of the other room and his mounting fear came not from this but from the sudden realization that there was no gun in sight.

Freddie had been shot, but there was no gun!

The killer still had it, and he, or someone else, was waiting.

An instant later Scott had his nerves in hand and the

panic had gone as swiftly as it came. He knew what he had to do, and he did it slowly and with deliberation, turning towards the front door, his face expressionless and a grim smile working at his eyes.

No telephone. Not now. Major Briggs would have to wait.

He opened the door and went out on the veranda. He closed the door behind him without looking back. When he started his car he raced the motor in case anyone was listening. He drove to a space just short of the highway corner, pulled in and cut his lights. The hand that presently lit his cigarette was steady.

He did not have long to wait. He heard the car coming up behind him, saw it pull on past and hesitate at the intersection before turning left and accelerating.

Scott did not get a good look at the driver but he thought he recognized the car, and its license number was firmly fixed in his mind as he stepped on the throttle. He had to wait at the intersection for a speeding car to pass but it was the bus that licked him. It was rolling fast, the ticket-taker clinging to the side rail, and he might have been able to cut in front of it had it not been for the car coming from the opposite direction. As it was he was held up. He had to sit there and watch the bus flash past and then he had to follow it. Because of oncoming traffic he had to wait behind it when it stopped to discharge passengers. When, a quarter of a mile farther on, he was able to get by, he knew his chance was gone and he slowed down, thinking hard, wondering what he should do first.

The thought of Sally made him turn left and start up the hill, using the road which skirted the golf course and wound upwards towards the bluff on which the

Crane house stood. In less than five minutes he was
swinging off the road and into the drive which led to this
massive, gray-stone structure which reared bleak and
foreboding against the night sky.

He saw as he approached that most of the house was
in darkness, the only light showing dimly from the draw-
ing-room windows on the right. There was no car out
front, no one on the wide veranda as he climbed the
steps. The front door stood open and he went inside
without knocking. A glance told him the drawing room
was empty and now, in the shadowed dimness of the
hall ahead of him he saw the telephone. It stood on a
small stand and on the shelf below there was a directory.
He did not expect to find Briggs at Headquarters at this
hour so he looked up the number of his residence.

It was when he started to dial that number that he
heard the noise. It was not loud, nor could he character-
ize it at the moment; but it was distinct enough to make
him stop dialing, to make him put the phone down and
go back to glance again into the drawing room. When
it remained quiet and empty in the half-light of the
single electric bulb, he crossed to the room opposite and
in front of the stairs. There was only darkness here, and
no sound but the hollow rap of his shoes on the polished wood floors.

"Hello," he said. "Anyone here?"

His words had an empty, artificial sound as they
echoed in the high-ceilinged hall and now, telling himself that what he had heard must have come from outside, he went back to the telephone and dialed his
number. Seconds later the Major's voice came to him.

Scott apologized for calling Briggs at his home. He

said that something had happened but first he wanted
to know about Waldron. Had Briggs found him.

"Oh, yes," Briggs said. "We took him off the *Colombie*
a half hour before she sailed. He did a rather clever
thing. Took a third-class passage. We very nearly
missed him."

"Where was he going?"

"He was booked to Cartagena."

Scott had it on the tip of his tongue to tell Briggs
about Freddie, and then he stopped. The sickness was
still with him, born of guilt, the thought still festering
that if he had listened to Freddie in the first place the
little guy would still be alive. Now, in his own mind, it
was no longer enough that he tell Briggs; he felt compelled to do something on his own, something that might
help to ease his conscience. If he could have a hand in
helping to trap the one who had killed Freddie it might
assuage the feeling of self condemnation. Even if he
failed it seemed terribly important that he try, and because there were things he had to know first he said:

"When did you pick him up?"

"Around four."

"Where is he now?"

"Oh, we've been holding him."

Well, that takes care of that, Scott thought, feeling
very little surprise now that he understood Waldron
could not be guilty of murder.

Aloud he said: "What does he say about Luther?"

"Oh, he corroborates that statement in part. When I
confronted him with that newspaper piece he admitted
right off that he was the missing Tim Welsh. He had
about twelve thousand, American, on him in cash. The

balance is no doubt in some deposit box in a New York bank."

"Luther saw him rowing back from the *Griselda?*"

"And Waldron admits he was out there. He got the idea from you at the Club Morgan. Julia Parks sent him the article as we suspected and then called him up from the Carib the night of her arrival. When you told him she was in the forward cabin he saw a chance to get to her alone so he drove to the Aquatic Club, found a skiff tied at that little landing stage and decided to appropriate it for a few minutes."

"Did he say *why* he wanted to see Julia?"

"Oh, yes. Said there was no telling what she might say when she was drunk and he hoped to make some sort of agreement with her before she got other ideas. He was willing to pay something for her silence and, in fact, had hoped to reach that agreement at Club Morgan; that's why he was waiting there. She'd promised to come but she didn't."

"Does he admit that he killed her?"

"Quite the contrary. He insists she was dead when he went into the cabin. It frightened him so when he realized his position that he was afraid to row back to the Aquatic Club—afraid someone would see him and remember—which is why he rowed directly to the beach where Luther saw him. . . ."

Briggs had other things to say about that meeting but Scott did not hear him. What he heard was something else, something that came not from the receiver but from somewhere in the house.

He did not know what it was but he was sure he had heard it. He waited for it to be repeated as he had waited for a repetition of that sound he had heard earlier. He

thought it came from somewhere in the rear or from below, and he turned, breath held as he listened, peering
into the unrelieved darkness at the back of the hall, neck
muscles tensed and his nape prickly.

The wind working on a loosened door? No. For there
was no wind. Nor was there any repetition of the sound,
only the metallic clatter of Briggs' voice in the dia-
phragm of the telephone. Scott put it back to one ear
and tried to listen with the other.

Briggs was explaining how Luther had arranged passage on the *Estelle* and how Waldron had hired the mate
to make sure Luther was aboard in time.

"Naturally he won't admit he was the one who struck
you from behind at the dance. That would make him
guilty of assault. Neither will he admit that he killed
Julia Parks . . . As a matter of fact," Briggs added, "I've
been in touch with New York by overseas telephone and
they say that Welsh—or Waldron—has no record of violence. Still—"

Scott was listening again for sounds in the quiet house.
He wondered if there could be a servant out back somewhere until he recalled that Crane had said there were
no servants sleeping in while his wife was away.

He remembered too about the massive construction
of the house and its thick-walled and vaulted cellars.
Then, deliberately, he closed his mind upon such speculations. He had found out what he wanted to know
and it was time now to get on with the job.

"I think Waldron's right," he said. "I don't think he
killed Julia."

"Really."

"I think Freddie Gardner knew what was going on
that night."

"You do?" said Briggs in a voice that suggested none of this was getting through to him.

"Freddie knew and Freddie made the mistake of telling the wrong person. I think the same person killed Freddie that killed Julia; it's the only way it figures."

"What?"

"And it couldn't have been Waldron because you've been holding him."

"But what's this about Freddie?" Briggs said, irritable now.

"He was killed tonight and not too long ago. Shot to death at his house."

Major Briggs was not a profane man but he knew the proper words and now he gave vent to them. He did a good job but Scott could not appreciate it because just then he heard the car start up somewhere behind the house.

In the next instant the motor raced and Scott, remembering how Freddie's car had been left out back the night before, understood that this car he heard had been there before he arrived. Someone had been lurking in the house, and he *had* heard a noise, and now, seeing a quick flash of reflected light skip across the ceiling, he jumped up.

"I'll call you back," he shouted. "I'll call you at Freddie's house."

Briggs was shouting too as the connection was broken. Scott had time to think that the Major was going to be very very sore indeed at this seeming lack of cooperation; then he was running through the door and across the veranda as a car roared down the driveway, only its tail lights and license plate visible.

Scott did the best he could. Leaping sideways off the

high steps he reached his little sedan in two strides. A
second later the motor was going and he was in gear. A
jerk at the wheel started him off just as the headlights
of the car ahead turned into the highway, and then he
was rolling downhill and making the same turn, not sure
he could follow the other car but fairly certain who was
driving it and where it was going.

20

THE ROAD was downgrade and winding and Scott
drove fast but not recklessly until he came to Highway
7. This was a stop street and he obeyed the sign before
turning left. For some distance here the road was
straight and he could see three cars in front of him before the curves started again. The one ahead was not
the one he wanted and he followed it for a half mile
before he could pass it.

He still did not know what was ahead of him but after
another half mile he came to this turn he was looking
for and cut right towards the sea. The shore dipped
sharply in here at one point and on the opposite side of
the resulting cove he saw headlights just disappearing
around the corner.

Inshore the water was a glassy black but farther out a
white line of surf broke upon a reef, and beyond that
and far down on the horizon a solitary light marked the
progress of some sailing craft. He saw all this briefly as
he skirted the cove and then the road swung left and
straightened into a narrow lane, lined with small houses

on the left and on the other side, the walled-in yards
of the more elaborate estates which faced the sea. Far
ahead of him a red light winked and went out and presently Scott slowed down until he came finally to the
gateway of this two-storied stone house, the front of
which overlooked the beach. When he saw the name on
the gate-post he knew it belonged to the Farrows.

Leaving his car parked just beyond the gate he
walked back and stood a moment, speculating, eyeing
the house across the road and remembering what Briggs
had said. It was here that the party was in progress the
night the Farrows had come home together; here that
some guest had seen a car come through the gateway
at a later hour.

There were three cars parked in the paved court beyond the wall and when he stepped close he saw the
familiar license number and knew he had come to the
right place. Somehow the knowledge did not excite him.
In a way this might be the end of the road but he had
no enthusiasm to explore what lay there. He felt tired
and strangely sick inside and it was this sickness and
his thoughts of Freddie Gardner, rather than any concern for Sally that made him press on.

Sally was all right. Sally would be all right unless
something unforeseen happened. That is what he told
himself as he walked past the cars and skirted wide to
the lawn on the right. The lights were on all along this
side and he could see someone working in the kitchen.
In the room beyond a maid was setting the table for
dinner and now, coming to the veranda, Scott climbed
the rail and tiptoed along to the room at the front where
light spilled brightly from open French doors.

By then he could hear voices and he moved quietly

forward, keeping to the wall until he could peer round the corner and get a glimpse of the room and the five people who stood there.

Until that moment Scott had not known what to expect. In his own mind, supported by his own brand of reasoning, he thought he knew who had killed Julia— and Freddie. He had hoped to tell Briggs what he thought but things weren't working out that way. The strain in the voices that came to him, the words that were spoken, told him that something quite drastic had to be done before Briggs could arrive. A man with a gun in his hand is not always amenable to reasoning and the spoken word, and now, understanding what was happening, Scott felt the tension build swiftly inside him. For it was all too clear that if anything was to be done in time it would have to be done by him, the occupants of the room being otherwise occupied.

An oversized coffee table in front of the divan was laden with cocktail things. Beyond it, near the mantel, Howard Crane stood beside Sally. Diagonally ahead were the Farrows: Vivian with a cocktail in one hand and her cigarette holder in the other, Mark, dark-haired and stocky-looking in his gray flannels, edging slightly in front of his wife.

"Don't be a fool!" he was saying.

The voice that answered him was high-pitched with strain and carried overtones of hysteria. It came from Keith Lambert, who faced away from Scott at an angle. In his hand was a small automatic pistol and it was pointed right at Vivian.

"I know what I'm doing," he said. "Just stay away from me unless you want to get hurt."

Crane cleared his throat. He gestured emptily, the

smile on his tanned blunt-jawed face as fixed and false
as a burlesque queen's.

"This is not the way, Keith," he said with surprising
calmness. "Let's get the police if you're so sure about
this."

Scott did not hear what came next because he was
concentrating on the problem at hand and feeling the
stiffness slide up the back of his legs as he measured the
distance from the door to Lambert. He thought four long
steps might cover it and now he stepped softly into view
of the others, putting his finger to his lips to demand
in pantomime their silence.

Even at that angle he could see that Lambert's thin
face was white and set and shiny at the cheekbones.
There was tension in every line of his neck and shoulder,
and the gun never wavered as Scott took his second step,
recognizing the odds but knowing no other way.

It was difficult to take those steps without making a
sound. He could feel his muscles draw taut and knotty
as he forced one foot in front of the other, lifting it,
balancing all the time on the rear foot and then putting
the first one down, not touching the heel. He had to
transfer his weight from toe to toe. He had to keep his
weight controlled and it seemed, somehow, a ludicrous
thing. It reminded him of comics he had seen in movies
as they burlesqued the act of sneaking up behind the
villain. The difference was that he had never been more
serious in his life.

He did it well too. He made no mistake. The trouble
was that eyes are hard things to control, especially
when surprised. Someone, he never knew who, gave him
away.

Some glance strayed and in it there was something

that warned Lambert, for in the next instant his head swiveled and his eyes opened wide. His thin, gangling frame recoiled visibly. He never actually turned his back on anyone but he half wheeled and then retreated a step so he could bring the gun to bear in any direction.

For an instant then his eyes had a wild, startled look. He backed away another step, his indecision a frightening thing to behold. Finally he found his voice.

"Oh, no!" he said. "Not quite, Alan . . . You followed me," he said, his voice near breaking. "Well, now you can stand over there with them. Move!"

Scott let his breath out and felt his muscles relax. He took three steps in the indicated direction, easily and with deliberation. This put him beyond Lambert but still apart from the others. He cocked a brow at the gun. He did not like the tightness of the hand that held it, nor the tremor that came to shake it from time to time, but when he spoke he kept his voice as casual as he could, as though none of this was very important.

"You were at Freddie's," he said. "In the hall closet —or was it a room?—with that gun."

"I only got there a few minutes before you did," Lambert said. "He was on the floor and I picked up the gun and then I heard you knock. I didn't know what else to do." He hesitated, lip quivering before he could still it. "You followed me to Crane's."

"I tried to but I lost you."

"How did you know I was there?"

"I didn't."

"Then why did you come?"

"I knew Howard had picked up Sally." Scott gestured at Crane and glanced at the girl. She stood very still, lips parted and one hand on her bosom. Her green eyes

seemed shocked and bewildered and though she looked
at him when he spoke he was not sure she saw him. "I
thought he might have brought her to his place. Why
did you go?"

"What?" Lambert swallowed and wet his lips.

"You went to Crane's too. Why?"

"Yes, I went there. I heard you call the police."

Scott turned to the others and began to explain how
he had gone to Freddie's and what he had done after
that. He spoke unhurriedly, ignoring Lambert for the
moment and trying his best to sound unconcerned. Time
was what he wanted. Time for reason to penetrate the
dammed-up hysteria which was warping Lambert's
thoughts.

"You still haven't told me why you went there," he
said.

"Because that's where I thought they were." Lambert
jerked the gun towards the others. "They said they were
going to Howard's for cocktails."

"That was the original idea," Crane said, and winked
surreptitiously at Scott to show he understood the reason behind all these questions. "We were going to my
place for drinks and then coming here for dinner. But
Freddie refused the invitation and so did Lambert—"

"And so," Vivian cut in, "we decided to have our
drinks as well as dinner here."

"Maybe now," Lambert said in the same tight voice,
"you know why I refused. Why I changed my mind
about investing in this island of yours. I may not be concerned about the scruples or the conduct or the ideals
of my associates, but I hope I'll never be a partner with
a murderer."

He glanced at Scott. "Freddie was my friend," he said.

"The best friend I ever had. She killed him." He looked at Vivian, his gaze hot and bright and somehow no longer quite sane. "Just like she killed Julia."

"Nonsense," Mark Farrow said angrily.

"How crazy can you get?" Vivian put her glass down, the cigarette holder beside it. She straightened and put one hand on her hip. She looked right at Lambert, and if she was afraid she did not show it. "Why don't you pour yourself a drink," she said acidly, "and stop being childish."

"Keith."

Sally's voice came softly across the ensuing silence. She waited until Lambert glanced at her and then she smiled. It was a strained sort of smile. The pallor showing through the smooth tan of her cheeks spoke of the effort behind it and Scott was very proud of her as she continued.

"No, Keith," she said in the patient, almost indulgent tone of a fond mother talking to her child. "You must be mistaken. Vivian wouldn't do a thing like that. She couldn't."

For a moment or so Lambert seemed to waver in his resolve. He glanced again at this girl he had liked so much. He brushed his tousled straw-colored hair back from his forehead with his free hand. There may have been an instant when a further plea by Sally might have turned the trick but before that happened Mark Farrow's blunt indignant voice destroyed the spell.

"Of course she couldn't," he said. "Vivian's been with me ever since six o'clock."

"Hah!" Lambert said, scornful now. "That's what you said the other night," he argued. "You said you went home together and stayed there. You said neither of you left this house and that's a lie because I saw her come through the main cabin that night. In a bathing suit . . . You thought I was asleep, didn't you?" he said to the woman. "You too," he said, not looking at Scott but speaking to him.

"You wanted me to pass out so I wouldn't bother Julia. You thought I would if I took one more drink. I was afraid I would too. That's why I only sipped it and pretended the rest. You took my shoes off, and my jacket . . . Well, I wasn't asleep and I hadn't passed out. After you'd gone I sat up. I talked to myself, trying to get up nerve enough to go in and wake Julia."

Once more his mouth trembled and he said: "I couldn't make myself do it. I was afraid. I hated myself but I couldn't help it. I stretched out again. I was still awake when she came into the cabin." He looked at Vivian. "In a dark blue swim suit," he said. "You didn't see me at first and then you stopped and looked at me. You thought I was asleep. You went forward. I didn't hear a sound and I kept on pretending I was asleep until you left. Then I went in and looked at Julia. She had that pillow over her face and head. She was dead."

He took a quick breath and said to Scott: "Then you came just after that. I watched what you did. I saw you take the keys from Julia's pocketbook. I didn't know what to do. I—I guess I fell asleep. I can't remember anything until you shook me that morning."

"What rot," Farrow said. "You're lying," he added harshly.

"No," Vivian said.

"What?" Mark stared at her.

"He's right," she said, her voice strangely quiet. "I did go there."

"Vivian!"

She did not seem to hear her husband. Her strong-boned face was impassive, but her mouth was white and the proud shoulders had begun to sag.

"I couldn't sleep after we'd gone to bed," she said. "I kept thinking of her. Hating her. Knowing she would spoil everything if she could. Finally I couldn't stand it any longer and I knew what I had to do."

There was no other sound but the monotone of her voice as she told how she had put on her bathing suit and a long dark robe, how she had driven as close to the club as she dared and then swam out to the schooner.

"I didn't stop to think of the consequences; I guess I didn't quite realize what I was doing. Even after I saw Keith on the bunk I wouldn't give up. I went into her room and looked down at her."

She stopped and wet her lips. She said: "For what was in my mind I certainly must be guilty."

Scott swallowed against the dryness in his throat and for some reason found it hard to break the silence that expanded through the room.

"She was dead, wasn't she?"

Vivian nodded. "I couldn't see too well but I saw the pillow. It was across her face and I moved it and then I realized she was not breathing. I took her hand and there was no pulse and then—" Her voice broke but she quickly controlled it. "I can't remember what I did then. I only knew I had to get out. Somehow I did."

"Just a minute . . . Please!" Lambert shifted the gun and his mouth was slack. He peered bewilderedly at Vivian and then at Scott. "Are you saying Julia had already been killed. I mean, before that?"

"Yes," Scott said. "And she wasn't killed by anyone who swam out to do the job."

"Alan!"

The sound of that voice surprised Scott and he had to glance round to realize that it was Sally who had spoken. She had moved closer to her step-sister, putting out a hand to reassure her. He recognized that gesture for what it was, but it was the look in her eyes that hit him hard inside. Those eyes were silently pleading for help. He had given her hope and she was waiting, expectantly and yet afraid lest some trick or empty promise shatter his hope.

"Are you sure, Alan?" she whispered.

He swallowed against the sudden thickness in his throat, grateful that what she wanted to hear was the truth.

"Yes," he said. "I'm sure."

"How do you know?" Lambert demanded, his tone suggesting he believed none of this.

"A swimmer's feet would have been clean."

"Clean?" Farrow's hard-jawed face was grim but his dark gaze held a baffled look. "Naturally they'd be clean."

"I saw the wet spots on the deck that Vivian had made."

"But—"

"A swimmer coming directly aboard from the water could not have brought sand with him," Scott said, and then went on to tell how he had gone below in his bare feet once he had awakened. "I'd swept up before I went ashore," he said, "but when I stopped outside Julia's cabin there was sand on the carpet. I felt it. There was more sand on the cabin carpet."

When there was no reply he said: "It didn't mean anything then. I felt it and somehow knew that sand shouldn't be there but all I could think about then was Julia. Not until tonight when Freddie made me think, when I knew he'd been on the beach—not until then did I realize that if there was sand in the alleyway and cabin —and there was—it meant the killer brought it from the beach. It stuck to his shoes after he'd rowed out. When he went below some of that sand fell off."

"What you're saying is that Vivian didn't kill Julia," Crane said finally.

"I'm saying Julia was killed before that by someone who came aboard from the beach." He hesitated, glancing from one to the other. "Maybe you don't know about Waldron."

"Waldron?" Lambert said. "How does he—"

"He came aboard that night," Scott said. "I'll tell you about it. It may take a while but you ought to know about him."

He had Lambert's attention now and that pleased him. He still did not like the look in the young man's eyes nor the way he clung to the gun. It scared him a little and he was hoping that if he took his time his words might work as a mild soporific which, if it did nothing to change Lambert's mind, might at least make him less alert.

"Waldron was a friend of Julia's," he said, "and she phoned him the night she arrived. Howard knows about that"—he glanced at Crane—"because Waldron was questioned the other afternoon when we were. Maybe the rest of you know too, but what you don't know is that Waldron isn't the right name."

He went on unhurriedly to tell who Waldron was and

why he had come to Barbados. He spoke of the newspaper clipping that Julia had sent him and then he went
back to relate the story of Waldron and Luther and the
plan which was to get Luther off the island and remove
him as a witness until Waldron felt safe.

"Julia intended to blackmail Waldron," Farrow said.

"That's the way it looks."

"And Waldron killed her?" Lambert asked in slow
bewilderment.

"He says not." Scott hesitated. "And if the one who
killed Julia also killed Freddie then it couldn't have been
Waldron because Briggs has had him wrapped up since
four this afternoon when they took Waldron off the
Colombie."

"But"—Crane frowned and shook his head—"you're
trying to tell us that Julia was killed by someone that
came from the beach, and Waldron did just that, but
Waldron didn't do it."

"That's right."

"Then—who did?"

"You," Scott said. "The way I figured it, Howard, after
I'd talked with Freddie, is that it had to be you or him
and Freddie's dead. That leaves you."

Crane started to laugh, then stopped abruptly. "You
are serious, aren't you?"

"You know I am."

21

FOR A MATTER of two or three seconds a shocked
silence settled over the room. No one moved; no one
made any attempt to speak. Everyone seemed to have
forgotten about Lambert and his threatening gun.
Everyone but Scott. While the others stared at Crane,
he moved a step closer to that gun, not knowing what
might happen but wanting to be prepared. As with the
others, there was astonishment in Lambert's gaze but
deep down the eyes remained hot and bright and un-
predictable.

It was Crane who broke the silence. He cleared his
throat with a chuckling sound and a grin began to work
on his tanned face.

"You're being ridiculous, Alan."

"Maybe," Scott said. "Maybe not."

"But what basis is there for thinking—"

"Let's start with the hotel. You searched her room."

"Suppose you prove it."

"The only way I can prove it," Scott said, "is by the
process of elimination. The police checked the Carib
Hotel the day after the murder. Briggs will tell you that,
as he told me. Briggs says that no one asked about Julia
that first night or made any inquiries about her room.
So, without inquiries, how would anyone know which
room was hers?"

He answered his own question when there was no reply. "You were the only one who could know without

asking, Howard. You met her at the airport. You took her to the hotel. Whether you went up with her, or stood beside her while she registered, you knew. And later when you wanted to search that room you had to wait until the porch was empty before you could climb to the window. You had to do it that way because you didn't have a key."

Crane waved the argument aside. "Assuming you're right," he said, "assuming I did go to her room, that hardly justifies your accusation of murder. What possible motive would I have?"

"All I can do is guess about that. You sent for her."

"I admitted that to Major Briggs. I told you why."

Scott nodded and told the others what Crane had said. "You thought if you got Julia down here she'd clamp down on Keith so he wouldn't put any money into this club of Freddie's. You didn't want the competition." Scott shifted his weight and said: "It was a good story. I believed it and I guess Briggs did too."

"It happens to be the truth," Crane said.

"I doubt it. I think there was another reason you sent for her but it didn't occur to me until this evening. I'll admit I'm guessing about this but"—he paused to glance about the room—"you can stop me if I'm wrong."

He looked at Lambert, found he still had the other's attention, and continued to Crane: "I understand you have a very pretty wife. I've been told she's not only lovely but rich. I think she's very important to your way of life."

"Agreed."

"You can play all the tennis you want, and sail your little sloop, and race your horses and fool around with things like the Surf Club. All on her money, Howard, because the way I get it you don't do a lick yourself and couldn't pay your own way on any of those things."

"Just a minute." Crane's face flushed and his eyes grew mean. "What happens between Mrs. Crane and myself needn't concern you."

"But it does," Scott said. "You want a motive for murder and I'm trying to give you one. You've admitted you were friendly with Julia last summer while your wife was in England. Everyone seems to know about that part of it. I think it was a lot more than friendship. I think—"

Lambert cut him off.

"How right you are," he said. "I knew what was going on. Three different times you and Julia went to Trinidad by different planes," he said to Crane. "I hired a detective in Port of Spain to be sure in case I ever wanted a divorce and Julia contested it. I never needed that evidence because by fall she had decided to get her own divorce. What she did last summer meant nothing to me but it would have to you, Howard, if your wife had found out just how friendly you were with Julia. She let you spend her money but she would have left you in a minute if she'd ever known how it was with you and Julia. And do you know what would happen then? You'd have ended up clerking in the grocery store."

He ran out of breath as he finished and Scott continued, speaking again to Crane.

"You knew where to cable Julia," he said. "If I'm going to guess I'd say she'd been blackmailing you by mail. She'd made a terrific mistake by divorcing Keith too early and it must have bothered her plenty. She'd settled for a little cash and a handful of jewelry when she might have been rich. She probably brooded about it and I think she finally came down here with a three-way plan in mind."

He hesitated, palms damp and the perspiration beginning to prickle on his scalp. The room seemed unnaturally hot and still and there was no sound but the muted crunch of the surf on the beach outside. Crane was waiting, gaze narrowed and his jaw set. The others were waiting too but he was no longer concerned with them. He swallowed and said:

"She had this idea of a colossal bluff she wanted to put over on Keith, hoping for some sort of a quick cash settlement before he discovered she was lying about the divorce. We know she expected to collect from Waldron, or Welsh, so why not collect a final payment from you while she was here? You'd have to pay and you knew it, so you sent for her, wanting her to come while your wife was away in Jamaica, planning all along to kill her, maybe not knowing how or when until you saw the perfect chance the first night."

"You're still guessing," Crane said.

"In a way," Scott said. "This is no court of law. It'll be a police job in the end and right now all I'm trying to do is answer your question . . . I say you had a perfect chance to kill Julia," he said. "The minute you saw me at Club Morgan you knew it. You knew she was alone on the schooner and you knew it would be a while before I started back. Waldron knew it a little later—you couldn't have missed him by much—and he tried the same thing. So everyone but you and Waldron and Freddie Gardner thought I was still aboard, Freddie because he hung around the beach too. I don't know why unless he was also trying to get up enough nerve to do what so many people wanted to do."

He wet his lips and said: "Julia was dead when Keith and I came back at one o'clock and no one in his right mind, believing I was still aboard, would have tried to sneak on until I'd had a chance to get to sleep. Vivian did wait. She and Mark drove home when they went ashore—that was around eleven twenty or so—and she didn't come back until about two. Keith came to Club Morgan just after you left so he had no time to kill Julia, and I know he didn't do it later because I took off his shoes; he couldn't have tracked sand into the cabin. Neither could Waldron because he did not come aboard from the beach. He came from the Aquatic Club pier. That left you and Freddie, and now there's only you."

He paused again, feeling the tension building up inside him and still afraid of what might happen. He sidled a bit closer to Lambert, still watching Crane and seeing now the grayness showing through the tanned skin, the shine of perspiration on the forehead.

"That's it, Howard," he said. "What did Freddie want, money? Did he threaten to go to Briggs?"

Lambert forestalled an answer. It seemed now that he had heard enough and he spoke to Crane, his voice ragged but surprisingly quiet.

"Step away from Sally, Howard!"

He gestured with the gun and Crane, seeing that wild look, obeyed. Then Sally, understanding finally what Lambert had in mind, cried out.

"Keith! Please, Keith! Look at me!"

"Now look here, Keith," Farrow snapped. "Put the gun down. Think what you're doing, man. Think, damn it!"

With that Scott got into the act. He tried hard in the

only way he could think of, hoping his voice sounded bluff, hearty, deprecating.

"Get smart, kid," he said. "What you need is a drink. Let's all have a drink and then we can sit down and talk this over and—"

"He's right, Keith," Vivian said, interrupting. "It's a job for the police now. Mark can call the Major . . . Go ahead, Mark!"

The telephone was no more than six feet away and Farrow moved towards it, one eye still on the gun. He glanced at Scott, who nodded encouragement. When he picked up the instrument Scott said: "Try him at Freddie's. He should be there now."

Lambert seemed not to have heard any of this. His gaze was fixed and beneath the thin, high-bridged nose his mouth moved silently and grew wet at the corners. To Scott it seemed that the other had nearly worked himself up to the last desperate, half-mad moment of decision, and Crane seemed to sense this. He backed away a small step and made a futile gesture with his hands.

"Easy, man," he said. "That's Freddie's gun."

"Does it matter?" Lambert said in a broken voice Scott had never heard. "Freddie was my friend. He never did a mean or vicious thing in his life. It wasn't in him to hurt anyone."

"I didn't go there to kill him," Crane argued. "He phoned me. I went to see him on my way to pick up Sally. He said he'd seen me row out to the schooner. He said he thought the police suspected him and he'd have to tell what he knew. I argued with him. I guess he had the wind up by then because he took out the gun and I grabbed for it. That's the way it happened."

Scott let his weight come forward and his arms swing down. He knew now that further argument was useless. In some ways Lambert had never grown up and he had lost temporarily all sense of reason and judgment. A slap in the face would have shattered the spell his mind had woven but Scott was afraid to gamble. When the gun raised two inches and the ridged knuckles tightened he leaned forward and slapped at the wrist.

He hit it as the gun exploded. A section of the window glass three feet from Crane dissolved in fragments. Then, as Lambert cried out, Scott struck him across the face with his open palm and, still moving in, knocked the automatic from his hand.

Lambert staggered back, his mouth open but no sound coming from it. Vivian swore under her breath. Then it was all over.

The gun, which had skidded fifteen feet across the floor, came to rest at Crane's feet. Before anyone could move he scooped it up, straightened, and swung the muzzle towards them.

For a long moment then no one moved and again the only sound was the intermittent crash of the surf on the nearby beach. It was Lambert who broke the spell. His face seemed to come apart and he covered it with his hand as he sank back on the divan, his sobs a dry, racking sound as reaction hit him.

Sally, who stood closest to Crane, merely looked at him as though at someone she had never seen before. Vivian's groan was an exasperated sound and Farrow, who had called the police but still held the telephone, put it down slowly.

"That won't do, Howard," he said. "That won't do at all. Surely you don't propose to use that on us."

Crane looked the room over, his flat-muscled body relaxed and at ease. His face was wet and shiny and the collar of his shirt was dark with sweat. For a silent second or two he seemed to consider the question; then he shrugged.

"I hope not."

"I mean, you can hardly expect to get off the island," Farrow said.

"No, I suppose not." Crane backed toward the open French doors. "I might try. I really can't say. All I know is that I need some time to think." He paused on the edge of the veranda. "Don't do anything foolish," he said, "like trying to follow me."

With that he was gone and Scott could hear his running steps before the silence came again. Then Vivian got busy, pouring whisky into a glass and sitting down beside Lambert. Outside a car started up, accelerated and was quickly gone. At that moment the dining-room door opened and a Negro butler appeared to announce dinner.

Vivian looked up, startled. "Oh, dear God, no!" she said wearily. "Mark . . . Do something about it, will you? Speak to Charles. Tell him—oh, tell him anything."

She turned back to Lambert, her voice soft now as she spoke to him, her manner solicitous. Scott walked over to Sally and took her hand. She went, unprotesting, as he led her to the veranda and the wicker furniture grouped at the front overlooking the sea. He guided her to the settee, and because his knees were still a little weak, sat down beside her. Then, not knowing exactly what to do and not yet trusting himself to speak, he resorted to a male gambit of offering a cigarette.

Neither spoke but presently he reached for her hand

and she let him take it. He felt the small shudder that ran through the arm touching his; he heard her sigh and watched her look out across the vague white line of breaking surf. When she was ready she said:

"What will they do to him?"

"If he's alive when they catch him he'll stand trial."

"But—will they—"

"That will be for the jury to decide."

"And we'll have to testify. All of us. Will we have to stay?"

Scott said he did not think so. He said if they gave proper and detailed statements it would probably be enough. Then she shivered again and he asked her what she was thinking.

"That it might have been me," she whispered, "if I had held that pillow down. I knew I hadn't and yet—if it hadn't turned out this way I might never have known for sure I didn't do it."

He did not tell her that it was some such thought that had made him do the things he did in the beginning but he felt the pressure of her hand tightening on his own. She held on as the lights of a police car swept the side of the house, highlighting the surf ahead. He knew they would have to do a lot of talking before the night was over but such things no longer seemed important. The important thing was this girl beside him, and he knew that whatever happened between them would be real and lasting and worthwhile.

He stood up, pulling her with him and holding her close for a moment. He smiled down at her. He said they had better go in before the Major sent out a searching party. . . .

www.ingramcontent.com/pod-product-compliance
Lightning Source LLC
Chambersburg PA
CBHW031405250626
47155CB00004B/1426